Should I Go On?

A

Novel

J.T. McNair

ISBN: 979-8-9940984-0-0

Cover design by J.T. McNair and J.L. Van Dyke

Dedications

To my mother, Jorene LeMay, who somehow gave me the joy of writing in 2022, and a staunch work ethic the day I was born.

To my *Muppet*, Jamie Lynn Van Dyke, who makes me believe I can do anything in the universe—regardless of reality—and cheers me on throughout all processes.

And to my children, Graycen and Margot, who are stunning in their intelligence, character, and beauty.

1

The Wind Up and The Pitch

Let me tell you a story. Some, or all of it, is true and it wasn't that long ago when it took place. It begins somewhere, anywhere, in Louisiana, where there is a television turned on. And on that television, a commercial break occurs to show the viewer something they would rather avoid than having to sit through.

As the advertisement fades in, an "adorable" elderly couple, actors of course, are seated at a kitchen table. She is gray haired with light make-up. The gentleman is just as gray as she, but, unlike many other men his age, he has a full head of wavy hair. He also sports a tan sweater vest adorned with big buttons. Underneath his vest is a blue cotton shirt. An entire length of chambray is shown where more tan sweater should be. His big stupid toothy grin at the ready as he breaks the fourth wall of the tv screen. His "wife" looks on with reverence for her "husband" as he begins the sales pitch.

"Ya know, me and Martha here," he motions to her with a mug of emptiness clutched in his hand, "well, we have been thinking that

4

we need a long cruise. Nothing would please me more than to take my bride on a long overdue luxurious vacation on a large ship. Heck! One of them that go around the world!" he continues to grin as he turns to her.

The script must have called for her to pipe up because here she comes with her shaky voice, "And Rupert, well, he did wonderful in his career. He also kept up with those payments on his life insurance policy to make sure I would be provided for should he…I don't even want to think about that," she finished as she rolled her eyes and shook her head as if she were trying to stave off tearfulness. Martha went on, "That policy made sense before the kids were all grown and on their own," she says as her dentures make an appearance. The elderly male actor looks of solemn hangdog pride and takes her hand. Slowly, the camera now closes in on her as she continues, "But now," she said with a shrug, "well now we can use that money to take that cruise without spending a penny of our retirement. Though, until recently, we didn't know it was even possible to do such a thing with that type of policy. We didn't know who to call or anything until I overheard the girls down at the beauty shop talking about it."

Rupert chimes in, "Martha did some checking around and it turns out that there is a company that will take over my life insurance policy and pay us a handsome sum. What a novel idea!" Had there been a drop of liquid in that mug he would have sloshed it all over poor "Martha".

"That's right, Rupert," she finishes with a giggle like she had done something naughty. "The people at S. L. Acquisitions were so kind to take my call and explain everything to me in simple terms that anyone can understand."

5

"Even me!" the male actor says goofily and points to himself like he was still standing on stage somewhere way off Broadway.

"Martha" feigns a laugh then crows, "It's amazing the price they quoted me for Rupert's policy. Then, they sent over the paperwork and, after reading over the packet, we just couldn't imagine how it wouldn't be one of the best financial decisions we ever made."

"Rupert" pipes up with his final line, "Now, we are all packed and ready to go! We're gonna live life with gustoooooo!" "Rupert" finished with more empty mug waving.

The commercial concluded with the two elderly love birds looking at one another like they knew a creepy secret no one else could possibly know just before the company logo overlay appeared and a quick word of legality from a disembodied voice closed the whole sordid thing.

The commercial couldn't have been cheesier. Nor could it have been more full of bullshit. Oh, it was true that S. L. Acquisitions, the S. standing for Shady and the L for Lane, would remove your beneficiary from your life insurance policy and add their company in its place. Not only would they keep paying the premium, but they would also pay the holder of the policy, you, a tidy sum. And who cares when you are going to die soon, anyway? Armored trucks don't follow hearses, you can't take it with you, right? But it's a morbid business model. They, and others like them, are companies that hope you died sooner rather than later so they can collect in full. What a novel idea indeed, "Rupert".

And so, over next several months, hundreds of thousands of Louisianian's and people in surrounding states saw or heard that particular commercial, and a few others like it, repeatedly.

Maybell Johnson certainly did but she wouldn't act on it, she loathed the plastic, fake, and pandering advertisement. She even shouted at one point, "I'M ELDERLY, NOT STUPID!" when she had enough of the back-to-back showings that were blocking her from enjoying her usual crime or news shows.

2

Maybell Makin' Groceries

On a grocery store aisle, a woman, who wore no makeup and was closer to seventy than she was sixty years of age in a flower print button down blouse and black "stretchy pants" with pockets stares intently at a few dozen choices of salad dressing. She's short, gray, and a little heavier than her cardiologist would want her to be— though she didn't give a damn and told him so. Maybell Johnson was doing what is known in some New Orleans circles as "Makin' groceries" in the Kroger supermarket located near her home in New Orleans East and not far from the Lakefront Airport.

After surveying several of the offerings that, at a distance, she couldn't read, Maybell reaches out and picks one up based on the color she knows she wants—white. But, as she pulls it closer, she can see dark specks in the mix. Already starting to grimace, she wants more information. With dressing in one hand, she picks up her reading glasses with the other and puts them on. The cheap, ornate, and dangly chain jiggles near her face as she perches the cheaters just at the tip of her nose and tilts her head back, training her eyes on the label at a near 90-degree angle.

"Now, let's see. Wadda' we got here?" Maybell said aloud, talking to herself in a questioning and hushed tone. Then slowly she responds to her own query while reading the label aloud quizzically, "Peppercorn ranch," Maybell pauses and shakes her head. Then, loud enough to be heard two aisles away, she exclaims, "Man, I wish they would quit messin' 'round and just make some RANCH!"

Maybell couldn't put the bottle back fast enough. She stayed bent over where the other types of dressings were located and squinted close to the other white bottles as she knew all she wanted was ranch, plain and simple. Once she located the dressing with none of those offensive peppercorns ground up in it and surveyed the label just to be sure it was the dressing she wanted, she placed it in her cart and went on about her merry way, gathering the rest of her wants, needs, and shouldn'ts. Under the shopping cart was a big bag of dog food that was placed askew and knocked into things here and there. Maybell was well known in that store, and it was evident when she got to the conveyer belt.

"Find everything you needed, Mrs. Maybell?" the chirpy check-out fella asked.

"Eventually," Maybell said with a huff. It was just then that a handful of wildflowers were slid just under her nose. It came from someone standing behind Mrs. Johnson.

"Here ya go, Mrs. Johnson," said Harvey Thibodeaux, the store manager. Harvey had worked there since he was a kid—stocking shelves. He worked his way up and when Mr. Boudreaux died, Harvey was poised and ready to take his spot.

"Harvey, get dem flowa's out my face!"

"Awwww now, Mrs. Johnson, don't you go bein' all cross. I think a nice young lady like yo' self should have a nice BOU-quet once in a while," Harvey said while looking over at "chirpy checkout fella" then mouthing, "These are on the house," he finished with a wink.

"Wellll, that's mighty kind of ya," Maybell quickly softened while surveying the bunch after she took them in her hand, "I know right where these'll go."

And when she got home, that's exactly where they went, in the trash. She wasn't being mean spirited about it. It wasn't like she didn't care about the kind sentiment. She just didn't like to be pandered to, she didn't like wildflowers, and she didn't have a vase that didn't already have something plastic in it that she liked better.

Maybell Johnson lived alone with her dog. Camille was a mutt that had wandered into the yard one day a few years earlier and never left. Maybell had only needed to feed her once and that was it. Camille was the only other living thing she cared about. Camille felt the same way about Maybell. The retired and elderly woman was independent, private, and liked it that way ever since Mr. Johnson had died of a heart attack nearly fifteen years earlier. She missed him more than life itself and would have prematurely joined him if she still thought about the afterlife.

For the last several years she often had darker thoughts than suicide and, at times, even enjoyed having them. The thoughts were about other people—those that she didn't care for—be they neighbors or just some clown on TV.

Mostly, though, they were about minor irritations and criminals. She also learned how to hide her darkness from everyone. Everyone except those who really got to her, but that was rare. Losing the love of your life will do that to a person; cause one to think darkly. If given the chance she would even act out in dark ways. Everyone has their limits, and everyone has the ability to take someone else's life, the only difference is the threshold. For some, it might only take a perceived slight or breach of etiquette. For others, it might take a threat to their life or the life of someone they loved; some might wish for their own end by their own hand.

Though Maybell found herself, most often, enjoying any story she could find depicting murder or some other debauchery, even laughing out loud at some of the darkness about the world, as long as they got the "bad guy". It had gotten to the point that even the news was too lighthearted for her, but she watched it anyway—it was mostly because the news was current and still had some mystery to it. Over the years, she had already consumed every ending to every murder mystery, real or invented, that had come along up to that point. She knew she had grown even more odd; different. She was still mad at a God she wasn't sure she believed in since the loss of her love, Ronald.

After putting up her groceries, including that plain ol' ranch dressing, Maybell fed Camille, "Ooo, girl, you gettin' fat… stanky ol' mongrel," Maybell remarked as she scratched her fur baby's ear while the dog was still eating. Maybell smacked Camille's left haunch twice to punctuate the sentiment. The mutt was none too bothered as she kept her head in the bowl. Nothing much stirred Camille. She was trusting of everyone; strangers included, and everyone was a stranger to Camille because she and Maybell kept to themselves. They were happy to live out their days in solitude and a guard dog, she was not. Maybell never felt the need to own one, anyway.

Once she fed herself a salad, Maybell settled into her retirement chair and turned on the TV to get a look at the crippled world she had watched grow darker since before she was a teen. She reveled in it, that darkness. Then that stupid commercial came on again.

Maybell awoke in the same chair she had plopped herself in, worn and ragged; both her and the chair. She had left the TV tuned to CNN. The ticker at the bottom shown what stocks closed up, down, or flat. She never played the market because she always knew what the deal was, and she knew she wanted no part of it. "Gamblin'-ass shit," she barked as she came out of her sleepy stupor.

The newscaster, one she never cared much for, was rambling on about some fire that appeared to be arson and took out a whole family. That was dark and got her attention—but only slightly. Her stomach got the best of her in that same moment. She entered the kitchen to make herself a bowl of cornflakes. However, before she took a single bite, she fed Camille again.

3

C-Suite

Maxwell Rutherford, an old money boy since birth sat behind an ornate solid wood desk larger than most people's dining table. He was sharply dressed in a pinstriped charcoal suit and red tie. Nestled in a high back leather chair, the well-groomed and coiffed man was also surrounded by groupings of high-priced collectibles; Katana swords, flint pistols in shadow boxes, and next to his tabletop humidor, a bronze bust of himself.

Maxwell had been the perfect CEO of Shady Lane Acquisitions since its inception four years prior—he created it. The owner now, though, was a shell company that had no known name. S. L. Acquisitions was but one of the many companies the ghostly empire owned and/ or decimated. They bought it from Maxwell after he had sold them a song and dance that made it attractive.

He quickly became the golden boy of the conglomerate of figures that made up a singular shadow. That shadow, that conglomerate, made its money from buying failing or up-and-coming companies only to sell them after a couple of years of returns. For the companies they ran into the ground, they would just dismantle them and sell off any assets. Rutherford, a master of monkeyshines got connected to this shadow through some backroom deals and discussions. However, S.L.A. was a company of his own design. Not bought nor stolen, but certainly not legitimate. Nearly a year ago, he sold his company, keeping only a 49% stake and went on to gamble with the shadow's money rather than his own.

At the front of that desk stood Maxwell's two lackeys. One was John Guidry. He had grown up on the scrappy side of the river, the West Bank of New Orleans. He was the shorter and smarter of the two. He said little and that's what made him smart. With a full beard, dark eyes and built like a fire plug, he also looked like a man not to be crossed—and few would. The few that did, regretted it.

The second, taller and stupid, was Abigail Siren. When she spoke, she was as shrill as her last name implied. She had lived all around—but mostly in Florida. She had moved to New Orleans a few years earlier. Since then, she had worked shitty jobs prior to blowing her way into this position; getting the opportunity to become a potential patsy should Maxwell need a fall-girl later on down the line. Her hair was long and dyed an odd shade of red, but it had not been done in a few weeks, and it showed. Already, the burnt locks were fading in a way that looked like someone had dumped a bucket of rust on her fat head. Her suit was tight, ill tailored, and didn't fit her well. But what did fit her well was the term "toady". Though, not just in position but in the way her mouth formed a sort of perpetual downturned line that always made her look as if she smelled something rank. She was not the brighter one and all three knew it, though she had been useful in some rather sordid ways over the last couple of years. She was boneheaded enough to take pride in that.

"So, I take it you two read the article I forwarded to you about the boomers living longer, no?" Maxwell asked while oscillating his gaze between the two.

Abigail piped up first, as usual, "Yes, but we can talk about it later. We have bigger issues."

"Bigger issues?"

"Yes!"

"Bigger issues than this company growing stagnant and the majority owners asking me questions?"

"Yes! Yesterday afternoon I spoke with, ahhh, what's his face…well the department that…"

"Financial?"

"Yes! Financial!"

Maxwell rolled his eyes and cut them at John who just shook his head.

"Anyway, financial…*Bill*, that's his name, *Bill* in financial...Look, Bill said that, well, I don't know how to say this, but, umm, people aren't dying fast enough."

Maxwell pounded the desk, "That's what I just fucking said, Abigail!"

John took over with a sigh, "Abigail, that's why he sent the article to us yester…"

Maxwell cut him off, "*I* know what the fuck that means, damn it! I don't need you two dimwits to have a conversation about that part with one another while I look on! What I need is a fucking solution and I need it yesterday!"

The two, John and Abigail, looked at one another and "shrill" decided, though it wasn't her idea and she wasn't sure she even understood it, that she would speak first, again.

"So, John has an idea," Abigail said proudly as if she were part of it.

John hesitated while his boss stared at him, waiting for something, anything that would move him to tears of joy, though, he wasn't holding his breath.

"Well, what the fuck is it, Johnathan?"

"Okay, so hear me out…it starts with Tor."

"Tor? The fuck? You mean the dark web?"

"Well, yes. The dark web is the start and end of the solution."

"First of all, what the hell do you know about the dark…you know what, never mind, I don't even want to know what you know or how you know it."

"I know a little…some...well, too much. Anyway, there are people who hold themselves out on there that will, ya know, take care of all kinds of problems."

"What sort of problems and how would that help us out? The fuck you think we are going to do, buy some untraceable…" Maxwell trailed off and thought better of finishing his sentence.

"Well, no…however, there are, umm, people who will…"

Maxwell put his fingers to his lips and pointed to the ceiling. He wanted his lackeys to get the idea that someone could be listening. His concern, of course, was "the shadow". He looked at both, oscillating again. He saw the glee behind the dimness of Abigail's eyes and the seriousness in John's. Then he looked out his 10th story window across the cityscape at the Superdome while picturing himself in a five-by-nine jail cell. Next, he had a vision worse than prison flash across his mind—the vision of his company tossed to the wind and him in poverty.

"The two of you said shit to anyone about any of this?" Maxwell whispered.

"No, of course not," Abigail shot back, and John just slowly shook his head "no".

"Good! Don't! I need time to think about what you are implying before I hear how the rest of this half-baked bullshit would play out. We should go to lunch at Galatoire's today. Clear the fucking schedule and we will talk there about it quietly."

"Oooh, I love Galatoire's!"

"Shush your face, Abigail! The both of you get the fuck outta my office. Call 'em up and reserve a private dining room."

4

The Neighbor

It was morning and Maybell and Camille went outside to get the paper, The Times Picayune. And, as always, there she was. The neighbor everyone has and nobody wants, Dorthy Gadfly. Dorthy was a woman in her sixties who didn't know it. Usually in tight white pants, tight shirts that, even though she was slight in build, showed off her implants that she had gotten in the eighties. And no matter the yardwork she was doing nor the heat she was doing it in, it never kept her from being in full makeup. Dangly earrings and long hair kept up under some big floppy hat always rounded out her look.

Maybell and Dorthy had been neighbors since before Mr. Johnson had died. He was a kind man and would speak with, even bring food to, Dorthy all those years ago. But she hadn't taken the hint that it was all Mr. Johnson and not Maybell that gave a shit about her, nor her cat, nor her ailments. Every time Maybell went outside to get mail, packages, or, like this morning, the paper, there she was waving and smiling and wanting to engage Maybell in conversation. If there was one thing Maybell loathed more than people, it was the idle chit-chat they tried to involve her in.

"Good morning, Maybell!" Dorthy chirped as she was watering her lawn. "How are you and Camille doing this fine morning?"

"Just fine, Gadfly, just fine." Maybell was never polite enough to return the question nor the sentiment. The Widow Johnson just kept face front and trudging along in her house coat and worn slippers, eyes staring straight ahead, and Camille in tow, looking for another one of her dark pleasures that she might find in the newspaper that lay before her.

As Maybell reached down to pick up the paper, Gadfly spoke up again, "Oof, I don't know how you do it, Mrs. Maybell. Ever since my back surgery, I just can't seem to bend down halfway to pick up anything."

"Yeah, I hear ya, Dorthy. I hear ya. Welp, it's too hot out here for me so I'll see you later." Maybell grumbled under her breath, "Like hell I will, last thing I need to hear about is the cyst you got removed off your back that you act like was a full spine replacement."

"I'm sorry, what was that, Maybell? I couldn't hear you. My ears ain't what they used to be."

"Oh, I was just telling Camille to com'on, get out this heat."

"Yeah yeah, it's hot alright, I nearly had a heat stroke yesterday." By the time Gadfly had finished the sentence, Maybell and her mutt were already in the house with the door closed.

Maybell spread the paper out on the table while Camille was eating her chow. Nothing too dark this morning. Just robberies, junkies, some federal trial and, as had become the usual in New Orleans, second- and third-page murder stories, always the same, no witnesses and no suspects. Someone got shot up in their car under the Grater New Orleans Bridge, better known as the GNO. Maybell had long since lost her sense of guilt over feeling disappointed that there wasn't something more sinister in the press, whatever the form.

"Well, Camille, just another day in paradise I guess, you ol' fat thing. I suppose we'll just see what's on the news at noon, maybe a good ol' fashioned drive by. Now that I think about it, we ain't had none of those in a while, huh ol' girl?" Camille just looked up from her half nap she had already started to take in the sunlight that shown through the side door leading to the kitchen of the old shotgun house.

"Humph, you ain't worth a shit, you ol' hound," Maybell said as she stood up and went over to Camille and rubbed her full belly then went to the stove to make her favorite—grits.

5

Galatoire's

"I'm Antoine and I'll be taking care of you this afternoon. What may I start you folks off with, today?"

"Do you have shrimp and grits?" Abigail asked.

Maxwell Rutherford had been gripping the chair since the wine steward had first shown up, and they had ordered Pinot Noir. He knew in advance what she was going to ask for. It was tradition at this point. He couldn't contain himself and they hadn't been seated for more than ten full minutes, "Abigail, you ask that every time! You know they don't!"

"Well, they should. Anyway, I could have sworn they did."

The male waitstaff spoke as if he were part of the conversation, "Ma'am, if I may without sounding too formal, shrimp and grits is known more as a, ahem, Lowcountry South Carolina and Georgia dish. As you may be aware, we are a New Orleans institution, and for over 100 years we have become and remained famous for our traditional dishes. However, shrimp and grits is not one of them."

Both, Maxwell and John looked over at Abigail as she kept her head buried in her cell phone while she spoke, "Then I will have the Sauteed Gulf Fish with Crab Meuniere," however, she came dangerously close to mispronouncing 'meuniere' as 'manure'.

Antoine responded with a stutter, "Eeeexcelent choice." It was clear he wasn't used to serving someone who was so unfamiliar with class, at least not with the higher end of it.

"And the gentlemen will be having…?"

Both responded in unison, "Filet, medium."

"No starters; turtle soup, Oysters Rockefeller?"

"No thanks, just the steaks, though I'll have a jacketed potato."

Guidry held up his finger.

"And you as well, sir, I take it?"

John just nodded with two quick pumps of his thick neck.

The three were seated at a table for twelve with Maxwell at the head and one lackey on each side, he opened the dialogue, "Okay, Johnathan, what you got?"

"Boss, here's the deal: we start small and maybe we stay small. We hire our problem solver from the dark web. We pick a random name out of our files. We offer the going rate and get the job done."

Shrill decided to exercise her pipes, "Won't that be suspicious if we do it a bunch? I mean, why would someone do that?"

"It's not time for that question…though, it's not a bad one. See, they will look like accidents; falls in the shower, stairs, fuck, I dunno."

"Fuck sake, John, are you kidding me?"

John looked Maxwell square in the eyes, "No, Max. I'm not."

Abby was already looking green around the gills. At least she was quiet for the time being.

John leaned in and continued, "Look you two, there can be no pattern. And if it doesn't look like an accident, meaning that, if something goes wrong and our 'fixer'," he used the air quotes when he said it, "screws up and has to, ya know, take someone else out in a way that makes it look like neighborhood robbery victims, that may be a good cover. They will be randoms that aren't on our client list but nearby."

They all traded looks at one another before John continued, "Not only that, but it's also not like we are the ones actually doing it. Those randoms, huh, we don't even give the fixer a name to go after," he finished with the wave of his hand. "Whomever we pay, they choose who gets clipped next, it just needs to be nearby the first problem. And we only pay cash, and they pick who the fuck they pick; hands clean."

"Hands clean my dick," Abby managed to say with a lump still in her throat.

"You got any better suggestions?"

6

The Cage

Maybell opened the door to Camille's cage that was located in a corner near a closet and the door just inside her bedroom, "Come on, girl, it's time fo' bed. Let's go." Camille jumped on Maybell's bed rather than go into the cage.

"Oh no you don't, you know betta than that. Come on now and git yo' narra ass outta my bed and into yours." The cage was lined with almost every bit of softness that Maybell owned. It was larger than it needed to be for a dog Camille's size. She was a medium mutt, part shepherd of some sort and a hound of some other. Black and gray with ears that could stand straight up or flop depending on her mood.

Camille looked as pitiful as she did every night she tried this; with her head down between her paws and grey eyes looking up, she resembled a knock off Hummel figurine.

"Girl, you know that shit don't work with me now com'on!"

Camille slowly climbed off the bed and slinked toward her cage. She was no guard dog and both ladies knew it. Maybell would just not have that dog sleep on her bed and it was the only reason she had the cage in the first place.

Maybell closed the crate after she patted the ol' girl on her back leg. Camille circled the cage twice and plopped down with a huff then looked at Mrs. Johnson with those same sad eyes.

Johnson did the same; plopped down on her bed with a huff and picked up a tattered copy of *Helter Skelter*, the book about the Manson murders. It was new when she bought it, but she had read it at least five times since then. Both drifted to sleep after Maybell cut off the light.

The following morning, Maybell did what she always had. She headed out to get the paper but tried to avoid Gadfly and, as usual, Maybell retrieved the Times Picayune while Gadfly attempted to get her attention.

"Mrs. Maybell, oooh, Maybell! Wait, let me turn this water off, maybe you can't hear me," Dorthy put the sprayer down and trotted over in her too tight white pants while taking off her gardening gloves. "I'm so glad I caught you this morning, yes indeed! You're not going to believe this but...."

"Then maybe you shouldn't tell me."

"No no, this is just too good not to share with my favorite neighbor!"

Maybell and Camille both stopped in their tracks. Camille looked at Maybell like she knew she was out of sorts and Maybell just looked at the ground and sighed then looked up in Gadfly's direction with a forced smile that shown no teeth, "Okay, try me."

"Okay, so you know that commercial with the ol' folks in it talking about…"

"Yes, I know that one with that ol' tired bastard and his silly wife lookin' at him like he won the Powerball."

"Yes yes, that's it!" Anyway, I called, okay, and, umm..," Dorthy said with her head on a swivel like she was trying to keep a secret then smacked the chain link fence with her gloves, "Well, look, it was super easy. I…I SOLD MY LIFE INSURANCE POLICY!" Gadfly looked around again and spoke in a hushed tone, "And they gave me a real good deal. They are the bees knees at that place. They were real nice like."

"Oh, I jus' bet they was."

"No, really, Maybell, they were just so helpful."

"Now you sound like you need to be in one of dem cartoon-ass commercials."

"Oh, now, Maybell, be nice…be happy for me. They said the check is on the way."

"Dorthy Mae, they jus' hopin', prayin, and bettin' that you gonna die sooner than later so they can get that big payout that your children have been waiting oh so patiently for."

"Aww now Maybell Johnson, that ain't nice."

"Naw, it ain't, but it's the troof."

"Pfft, well, that's just fine. I was gonna give you a year subscription to that ol' rag of a paper you read but, well, you're just being cross."

"Nope, just realistic," Maybell finished as she began to walk back into the house and grumbled under her breath, "Gamblin'-ass shit."

"What was that, Maybell?"

"I SAID GOOD FOR YOU!" And with that, Maybell slammed the door shut. Dorthy took a bit of satisfaction knowing that she had just got under the ol' widow's skin. Gadfly was just being a braggart, and a poor one at that.

So, Maybell did what she always did after scanning the front few pages of the paper. She went right to the obits. She liked to see how old the people were who died. It gave her hope and pleasure when she saw how young some of them were and that she had made it to the age they hadn't. And then it gave her some thought about how old she might become when she saw the age others were. Like people in their nineties made her wonder if she even wanted to get that old. However, looking at the pictures of the decedents was one of her favorite things to do.

"Ooo, Camille, look'a dis ol' buzzard." She flashed the picture to Camille. Maybell read for a moment then continued, "Man, it says here that he left a wife and five kids. I'd love to get a gander at who bedded down with that nasty thang. And at least five times, at that." Maybell couldn't imagine being married to anyone other than her

Ronald. That got Maybell to thinking about what picture she would want for her obit and who would even send it in for her.

Maybell went into her bedroom closet and pulled down a banker's box. She carefully opened the top while Camille sniffed around and peered inside. There were stacks of pictures and a few albums. Maybell began to leaf through them all. Her and her first and only love, Mr. Ronald Johnson stood there with her, arm in arm, on their wedding day. He was handsome and she was thin and curvy in her white wedding dress. A huge wedding cake was in front of the couple. It was clearly the early sixties. Both had smiles like they had waited their whole lives for that picture to be taken. She smiled back at it, and at him. Only Mr. Johnson had ever made her darkness slumber, and he did it for decades, and he did it effortlessly.

That picture and the rest made it clear that no one had taken a single photograph of her for years. At least none that she had in her possession. She didn't want her obit to read how old she was and then have some youthful picture presented in the paper. *Grow old gracefully*, she thought. But she also wanted to still retain a sense of dignity. She wanted to be shown how she was now, though, a little more put together. She thought of what it would be like had she asked Ronald to take the picture for her. But Ronald wasn't there to do so, and Maybell wouldn't let anyone else get close enough to do it— not in her space nor in her heart.

7

Maybell And The Mall

The next morning, Maybell went through her usual routine: get the paper, attempt to avoid Gadfly, feed Camille then herself, and read the paper while sipping her coffee. However, this day would turn out to be different than most, and different in most every way possible. To start with, the day before, Maybell had decided it was time to begin her preparations.

As a start to her unusual day and all the unusual activities that were to follow, Maybell sat herself in front of her rarely used vanity that lived in the corner of her bedroom. It was used as most surfaces were in her house; a place to set piles of memories, both useless and precious. After clearing off a small space on her vanity by simply placing the stacks on the floor, she opened the tri-folded mirrors. Surveying her face, side to side, she whispered to herself, "Ol' ti'ad lookin'-ass."

Rifling through the vanity drawers, she found some makeup she had not used in years. It had been so long she couldn't remember the last time she used any of it. Sticky mascara, crumbly lipstick, clumped face power from years of humidity. Maybell looked at each item as she huffed and grumbled to Camille who laid there and only reacted to her master's noises with a flick of one ear until she raised her head after hearing the vanity drawer slam shut.

Maybell got dressed in her favorite type of clothing; black "stretchy pants" with pockets and another faded flower print button-down blouse. She grabbed her purse, kissed Camille on the snout, hopped into her brown 1999 Oldsmobile Cutlass and set out to the Lake Forest Plaza mall. She was going to go there anyway prior to her realization that her makeup had long ago succumbed to the New Orlean's heat and humidity. The difference was now she needed to have herself "done up" by someone else. There was only one hitch in her plan, it was dealing with people. And to make things worse, it was people touching her while they attempted small talk.

Driving was not one of Maybell's favorite things to do. As a matter of fact, most things that took doing were not her favorite nor even tolerable. Even though the Widow Johnson was considered by most standards as "elderly", how she drove was not one of those standards. If she liked the Beach Boys, and she didn't, she would have considered herself like the *Little Old Lady From Pasadena*. Though it was true that her eyesight wasn't what it once was, Maybell had no problem remaining ten miles over the speed limit. She wanted to get where she was going and get back home as quickly as she left it. Being out and about was not an activity that Maybell considered a hobby. For her, the mall was the worst of the worst. She didn't like shopping, she didn't like spending money, and she didn't like people. The mall was about as full of everything Maybell considered her least favorite things.

Johnson's blood temperature, at its baseline, ran hot. And there were often situations in her world that would send it to stratospheric heights. Her progress toward any goal she set out to achieve being impeded by stupidity, laziness, or outright attempts to stymy her free movements would likely put her in the hospital with a stroke if she weren't, "bad grass". Mr. Johnson often joked with her about death. She would always respond with, "You can't kill bad grass." Maybell considered herself just that.

The widow was already irritable about having to add a makeup session to her list of items she need for her preparations. The time it would take and the banal discussions she would have to endure was on her mind at the time she encountered a left-lane hog.

The old Datsun mini truck in front of her had what Mrs. Johnson like to call "a history". That meant that it was dinged and dented, and this truck even had panels of other replacement parts that were the color of the same model truck it was taken off of at the local "Pick-a-Part" junkyard but clearly not original to this vehicle. This one was going right at the speed limit in the passing lane.

"Aww, here we go. Dis motha' fucka' gone ride this lane like he own it," Maybell could feel her ears getting hot as she started to press the brake pedal. "MOVE! WHIT CHA' RAGGETY ASS PIECE OF SHIT! OO-A-OO, I CAN'T STAND DEEZ SLOW LEFT LANE BASTA'DS!"

The truck was loaded with bumper stickers, old and new.

"YOU GOT ALL DEM STICKERS ON THERE TO HOLD THAT BUMPER ON? JUST LOOKA YO TRASHY SHIT! ALL BEAT TO HELL! Ya know what, someone need to check yo' truck fo' drugs. Probably high as a kite. To'w up from the flo' up and twisted like a pretzel. Punk-ass bitch. MOVE!" Maybell laid on the horn, but the truck went no faster, nor did they get over into the right-hand lane, not even when she flashed her brights at them.

Maybell continued to flick the stick on her steering column that made her high beams pop on and off a few more times but the truck didn't take the hint. Putting on her right blinker she stomped the gas pedal and went around. As she did, she slowed and gave a glaring look at the driver of the Datsun, "Lemme see what 'stupid' look like," she said aloud but only to amuse herself. The left lane hog didn't even look over. Both of his hands were gripped at the ten and two position and face forward like he had no idea at all he was irritating ol' Mrs. Johnson.

"Stupid ass," Maybell mumbled and made sure to get back in the left lane just missing his front bumper as she merged. The Datsun jerked as he jammed on the brakes to keep from hitting the Oldsmobile and Maybell relished her small victory while looking in her rearview mirror. "BRAHAHAHAHAH, YEAH, YOU DON'T LIKE THAT SHIT NEITHER, DO YA, CHUMP ASS MOTHA' FUCKA'!"

Maybell made it to the mall near the Dillard's entrance without any further affronts or impedance to her progress, parked, and locked her car. She had decided earlier while sitting at her vanity that she would go straight there and have a "complimentary"

32

makeover for the picture she was going to have taken for her obituary. She had learned some time ago that if one were to just act interested in some sort of makeup, there were technicians who would happily paint your face in the hopes you would buy some of the products they used.

Mrs. Johnson walked through the Dillard's doors and could smell the leather wafting off the purses and shoes she passed on her way to the makeup counter. Taking in the smell of newness and quality was a simple pleasure she allowed herself to enjoy, though, she had no plan at all of buying any of it. No one would see a purse or shoes in an obituary headshot. *Well, maybe a new belt might be nice*, she thought.

As she approached the counter, she now smelled the perfume and colognes that were segregated by the aisle she walked down. She smiled with a little delight as she found herself on the men's side. Mr. Johnson's favorite to wear was Devin by Aramis. She looked to her left, then her right, to see if any of the salespeople were waiting to swoop in and try to make a sale for something she had no intention of buying. Mrs. Johnson picked up the sample bottle and sprayed it on the thin plastic sampling wand she had found in a cup near the sample station. Mr. Johnson's little Mrs. May drank in the smell of her Ronald with her eyes shut and a smile on her face. When she came to from her trance, she slid the memory in her purse.

With her love and romance still on her mind, May turned her attention to the opposite side of the aisle where the ladies fragrances were and did what she did best, feigned a look of confusion to gain the trust of all the youngsters that began to take an interest in her and think about what they might be able to sell ol'

Maybell Johnson. Bending herself at the waist and putting her chained reading glasses up to her face, Mrs. Johnson surveyed the fragrant offerings, but not because she wanted any of them. It was because she wanted to be noticed.

"Hello, ma'am," one of the attendants greeted her with a smile. "What may I help you find today?"

"Oooh, I don't even know. I'm juss lookin' 'round, ya know. I mean, I don't even know why I might wanna try any of this new type makeup they got out here today," She said as she let her glasses fall to her chest and pointed over to the lines of makeup. "I've been usin' the same ol' stuff for years. Church, ya know. I mean, I don't wanna be going in the Lord's house lookin' like..." Maybell leaned in after looking over her shoulder and whispered, "...ya know, a hussy." That got a giggle out of the young saleslady.

As both women shared a laugh and a hand covered smile, the attendant walked Maybell over to the lines of makeup and said, "Oh, no ma'am, not in the Lord's house. Never that."

"Ya see," Maybell continued, "I have started to run low on everything and they have these TV commercials talkin' 'bout deez wrinkle creams that make people look younger. I mean, I ain't worried much 'bout all that but maybe that lipstick that won't come off on yo' tea glass might be nice. I mean, I wouldn't even know where to start and I don't even know how it might look on a woman my age."

"Oh Miss..."

"Mrs. Johnson but you can call me Maybell if ya like."

"Mrs. Maybell, I do believe I can be helpful."

34

"You could? You would do dat fo' me? Oh, bless your lil' pea pickin' heart. I juss knew when the Lord brought me in here today, he was gone send me to the right person."

"Mrs. Maybell, lemme tell you something, they don't normally do this anymore, management says it ain't worth it, but you are jus' the sweetest thang. You jus' come right on over here and sit in this chair." The young attendant brought her over to a black and silver swivel seat that had a thick bar at the bottom one could pump and make it rise.

Maybell sat her purse at the base of the chair then asked, "And what's yo' name you lil ol' sweet thing, you."

"Amanda, Mrs."

"Amanda...awe, bless yo' heart, that's my grandbaby name."

"Aw, I love that."

"Yes, inDEED I just knew the lawd's guidin' hand led me to the right person and I was correc'."

"Yes, ma'am, He sure did! Now, you go right on 'head and settle yo' self in and we gonna fix you right on up with some products that I jus' know you are gonna find to be jus' as classy as you are, Mrs. Johnson...uh, Maybell."

"Oh good, I'm actually so excited. Oh, and please make sure the mascara is the kind that don't do none of that runnin' cuz I jus' get so emotional durin' service. When I get the Word, I just be ballin' and squallin' and havin' a fit!"

"Yes, ma'am, we gonna' get you all fixed up."

Nearly a half hour later Maybell Johnson had a face that she was happy with.

"You just look classy, Maybell. Ooo, I know it ain't right in the Lord's House but there are goin' be so many of the other ladies who will be envious."

"Oh lawd, naw, now you jus' stop that," she finished with a giggle.

"Now, how many of these products might you like to take home with you because I jus' need to say, they all look great on you!"

With a big grin on her face, she looked right at Amanda and said, "Ya know, I'mma take 'em all! Would you do the kindness of puttin' them in a bag and leave it behind the counter? I hate to carry all that 'round. Dis mall is jus' so big and I don't like to show off with bags and what not. I have some other things I need to collec' before I come back here and get deez items. My car is right outside. The other things I need are lightweight. I'll come back by after I stop at the ATM and get the other things I still have to get because I like to, ya know, pay in cash and I forgot to stop by the bank. I'll be back 'round an hour or so from now. Would that be okay?"

"Oh yes, that would be jus' fine. Don't you worry none about a thing. I'll have it all wrapped up and ready for you, Mrs. Maybell. You have been jus' such a pleasure."

"Thank you so much, dear heart. See you soon," and off Maybell went. A nice dress was next on her list.

As much energy as those thirty-five minutes of small talk had taken out of Maybell's emotional bank, she had no intention of stopping by the ATM to pull money out of her financial one. She had the look she thought would be classy enough for her picture in the paper. She almost felt guilty. She quelled any shame she may have felt by simply telling herself, *They throw half of that shit out that they use as a sales ploy after each day and probably test on little bunny rabbits, anyhow.* That's all it took. Insofar as Amanda's time, Maybell noted to herself, *It's a good lesson for every young woman to learn not to be taken in by a kindly little ol' lady. Po' thing, she was nice, though.*

The women's clothing section in the D.H. Holmes department store on another side of the mall was next on Maybell's mental list. This time, however, she wouldn't try and con anyone out of their time nor product. Matter-of-factly, Maybell simply pushed through the lines of dresses on rack after rack. Some too loud, some to short, and some were both. She hadn't put much thought into what style of dress she wanted to be pictured nor buried in. As she thought more about it, she didn't know if she cared enough to be buried at all. For all Maybell cared, she could die somewhere and never be found and it would be fine with her. It was mostly how her tiny square picture in the obituary section of the paper was going to look. And she also knew it would only be in black and white. Her make-up wasn't for color; it was to contour her look. Whatever color dress she chose didn't matter much to her, either. In the obit picture it would only show as light or dark and she didn't care who would be there to see it while she laid lifeless in a coffin. *No one*

would be at my funeral except for Gadfly to dance on my grave. Ol'
fawnky-ass, Maybell thought in words and in pictures.

She went on thinking and flipping through dress choices. None
of them struck her fancy. She knew she had been lingering too long
and would garner the attention of a helpful and irritating
saleswoman; she was right. A blonde in her mid to late-twenties,
nicely dressed, and well-groomed approached.

"Hello, ma'am…"

Without turning around Maybell answered back before she could
even be asked, "Do you have anything like a pantsuit?"

"Oh yes ma'am. Let me walk you over Ms…"

"Mrs. Johnson, and your name is?"

"I'm Vicky," the saleslady said happily as if she had already
made the sale.

"Aww, ain't that something. My niece is named Vicky."

"Oh, that's nice."

"Ain't it, though?"

"Mrs. Johnson, I think we may have what you are looking for,
what color are you interested in?"

"Oh, just point me in the right direction, I don't need no help."

Saleslady Vicky was a bit taken aback and simply answered,
"Umm, okay, yes ma'am," and pointed over to a rack on the other
side of the store.

Maybell walked over to the rack that was built into the back wall and said nothing more to Vicky. She picked up a few red pieces then wandered over to a section of blouses and picked a few white and cream color ones. She knew she already had the shoes she wanted so at least that wasn't on her mental list.

In the changing room, Maybell put together her outfit fairly quickly and wore it out of the changing area. She held the tags that she had removed from the items she was wearing in her hand and left her unchosen items in the dressing room, making sure to take her favorite stretchy pants with her. *Fuck that dingy ol' blouse*, she thought as she left it with the other store items.

The attendant at the register asked if she had found everything alright and Maybell just nodded and said, "Sure did. I like this outfit so much Imma wear it right on out the store. That'll be jus' fine, right?" she finished by placing the price tags on the counter that she had removed from the red pantsuit, white blouse, and black patten leather belt she was now wearing.

"Oh, well, um, sure yes, that's plenty fine."

"Oh, thank ya so very much."

After paying for her purchases, Maybell Johnson walked out with her favorite stretchies in her D.H. Holmes bag. Her white tennis shoes didn't match anything but her new blouse, and she didn't care. What she needed now was a little black hat because she wasn't about to get her hair done. Maybell didn't want to have to sit and, either listen to someone talk her ear off, or fight her urge to comment while two or more other woman chatter on about their "no-good-ass boyfriends and/ or husbands". She didn't like anyone playing in her hair any more than she did in her head—but first a trip to the restroom was required.

Maybell had been to the Lake Forest Plaza mall a few times over the years and had figured out what restrooms were single person only. She was a private woman in every respect and easily irritated should someone encroach on that privacy. "Private Potty" was, without a doubt, one of those most sacred times.

She already knew, however, what was going to happen once she got into that bathroom because it always did. But nature was calling and as much as she disliked public restrooms, she had learned the hard way more than once as she got older not to pass one up.

Maybell made her way to the up escalator and ascended to one of the most private bathrooms she knew of; it was a single person restroom that locked. Out of all the unpleasantness that the whole mall process brought, this bathroom hideaway was her favorite. *The best of the bad*, Maybell thought.

She started her usual process by knocking and then put her ear to the door. She heard nothing. Then, continuing her ritual, she slowly pushed down the "L" shaped handle on the door. If her knock wasn't heard or if she didn't hear anything from a fellow "Private Potty" user on the other side, maybe the moving of the handle would work to alert them before either were embarrassed by seeing things that Maybell though ought not be seen. Also, if it were locked, she would be able to see the bolt not move from the space between the jamb and the door. This was a process that she took very seriously no matter what side of the door she was on.

The handle went all the way down and the bolt slid out of the jamb, meaning that it wasn't locked. But that didn't mean there was no one in there. Now the final step of the process was at hand. Maybell slowly pushed open the door. It was the last possible chance that if someone in there had missed all the cues, this one would surely do it.

No shriek, no yelling, no sink noise. No noise from any other orifice that could be in that room came out. Maybell pushed the lock button before she shut the door then checked the handle from the other side. *Yup, it still locks*, she thought happily, *It's the small things in life.*

Maybell took a moment to remove as much as she cared to in the way of her new clothing and carefully hung them on the hook on the back of the bathroom door. She liked to be as comfortable as possible while doing her business. However, this was not her home. So, as always, she decided not to get *too* comfortable.

Mrs. Johnson reached into her purse and retrieved her billfold where she kept all her receipts and made her way over to the *business doin' place*. There, she found that there was only one seat cover paper in the holder above the commode. She pulled it out carefully, but it ripped anyway when it snagged on the rusted metal paper holder. "Gotdayumned shitty-ass paypa'," she exclaimed, "Someone have mercy!" She struggled with the flimsy and torn apparatus. As she tried to place the paper over the seat of the commode, the center of it was hanging down and touched the top of the water, began to soak, and pulled the paper right into the pot.

"Aww, fuck it! Anything Imma get off the rim of this commode would eat right through that flimsy-ass shit, anyway." Maybell

41

settled in and began to do what she needed to do while rifling through her receipts collected over the past few hours.

Suddenly, the handle on the door went up and down several times in quick succession and the door even lurched as if someone had put their shoulder to it like a linebacker.

Maybell watched her suit jacket that she had hung on the back of the door land right on the filthy bathroom tile and that was it. Mrs. Johnson went right to Maybell mode in a quarter-second flat.

"SOMEONE IN HERE! DA FUCK WRONG WICH YOU PEOPLE? DON'T FOLK KNOCK NO MO'?"

The movement stopped and she could hear someone mumbling as they walked away. Maybell was so irritated she left her business half done, cleaned up, and surveyed her blazer she had picked up from the floor. Satisfied that she was lucky that there was no staining on her garments, she dressed, washed her hands, and went out to see if she could get a glance at the offender.

And there he was, a man in his fifties, gray hair and wide gray beard, just standing there with a pissy look on his face like he had been the one who was wronged. His hands were in his jean pockets as he stood waiting for whomever had been yelling at him on the other side of that door to come out so he could glare at them.

Maybell was not intimidated in the least "Da fuck you lookin' at? Oh no indeed! I ain't the one! You wrong fo' dat! Tryin' to come in there like gangbusta's then got the nerve to stand there and look at me like I'm the one bustin' in like the Kool-Aid man. And the woman's bathroom, no less. Well, I guess you need to get in there

42

and get to it before you shit dem dungarees you got on. Ol' Grisly Adams lookin'-ass!"

The man was slightly stunned and went to speak but Maybell was having none of it, "Don't even fix yo' mouf like you gone tell me shit. Teeth look like you been chewing aquarium rock. Get that shit fixed as soon you leave here today. Face all jacked. Mouth just full of mistakes," she finished as she started walking. The man said nothing and went into the bathroom where found a gift that Maybell had left him for causing her all that trouble.

The widow made her way to the down escalator to find a store that had a suitable hat. It didn't take long, and she didn't even have to make small talk with anyone. She settled on something petite and simple. She didn't care for large, brimmed hats. Now it was time for her big moment; to take a suitable picture.

Mrs. Johnson, with still fresh makeup, red pantsuit, black hat and belt, and bright white tennis shoes walked into Sears. When she walked past the appliance hawkers in suits, like it was still 1959, she simply put up her hand because she was still salty from her near bathroom break-in and said, "Don't need shit," and kept marching forward toward the family photo shop before the salesmen could get their greeting out.

There were two families ahead of her. They were all dressed in their Sunday's best. The kids were mingling with each other around a table that held multi-color wooden beads on a series of skinny, loopy, metal rods and all being as loud as a group of children could be. All Maybell could do was grumble to herself. Not only did she already surmise that this was going to take the rest of the day, and she wanted to get home to Camille, but she was going to have to put up with rowdy children getting in her space while their mom looked only at her phone and not at her children. Then there was the grandma, looking at the children with pride who would likely try to talk to Maybell. What was worse was that the waiting space was almost non-existent in size.

Maybell looked on with disgust when one child sneezed then wiped it on the side of the game table. He just continued moving around the beads as another little boy in a crooked clip-on bow tie kept trying to push his hand away, the same hand that had the lingering snot on it.

As she scanned the room, there were sample pictures that were of real families. They looked to be from the local area as they felt familiar to Maybell. Not in personhood but in local style. She just figured that folks had given permission to have them hang there. Some were clearly engagement pictures, some were of entire broods, and some appeared to be single-parent families.

One of the groups was called up and that settled things down a little, at least. Maybell sat with her purse and shopping bag clutched in her lap and over her belly. She had avoided any eye contact from everyone in the room. A little girl, maybe age four, and in a white Easter-looking dress sat quietly. Both ladies caught eyes, and Maybell turned away. But the little girl didn't; not one bit. The Widow Johnson felt as if she were being looked at so she side-eyed the little girl to see if she was. When she did, the little one formed a small and shy smile. Maybell smiled back and her heart was slightly warmed.

In an instant she was brought back to 1960 when she and Mr. Johnson had the discussion once, while they were dating, and never had it again. The conversation almost all partners have about possibly having or adopting children once they get married. May wanted nothing to do with it and made it clear but in a nice way to her love. Ronald wasn't going to argue but May never asked if he wanted any. She never knew if he was just going along with her or if he was maybe relieved because he didn't want children, either, and took it as lucky that she didn't. Her reasons for not wanting them came from a place of trauma and not practicality.

Ronald Johnson came from a medium-sized family by New Orleans and southern standards, and Maybell was an only child for most of her life. Her father went somewhere and never came back. Her mother worked two jobs and slept when she could until she slept all the time and then slept for good. Maybell found solace in playing with numbers. Not dolls, not toys, not even really doing much that was childlike after she started school. She took care of herself, and her mother liked it that way. Not because she didn't love May; because she absolutely did and May knew it 'til the end of her mother's life. May's mom just didn't have the time nor skills to be a tender mother. Then, tragedy struck and made things worse. Not having it to give, not being able to show it, and not having the luxury of money to have the time to practice it, meant May never learned how to care for another little human being, except herself. She was self-sufficient by age eight.

By third grade, May had a few other kids working for her in the schoolyard. May's mother had bought her a bag of Tootsie Rolls for one of her stocking stuffers. But May didn't eat them and when school was let back in after the Christmas holidays, she decided to sell them; three cents apiece or two for a nickel. After she sold the first bag's worth, she could buy three more bags the next time her and her ma went to the store, and she did.

Maybell never had many friends. She had a few people she allowed to get close to her before she got burned by a few of them. However, a few felt like so many to Maybell that by her twenties she had written off most everyone in the world. However, when a few of the kids wanted to get in on the action but didn't have any seed money, Maybell gave three of her friends each a bag of Tootsie Rolls. For every three penny's worth they sold, she got two cents, and they kept one. This went on for almost the rest of the school year. Near the summer break, it took her but one bag's rotation to figure out that two of the three were pinching off the top, and that was the end of that. She took counting and loyal very seriously.

May didn't like children even when she was one because she grew up so fast, she never felt her youth. Ronald helped her feel free like a child for years. She was so focused on him, and them as a pair, that she didn't focus on all the negative in her past and in the world that fed her darkness.

But since his passing, it grew back like a cancer; slow, methodical, quietly, and deadly. May wondered, while she was smiling back at the little Easter Sunday-dress girl, if a child—a daughter perhaps—would have made her dark cancer better or if it would have made it worse. Possibly better because she would get to live though that daughter and the two would have shared Ronald in common. Or, perhaps worse, because of all the bad things in the world and what one must do to help a child navigate them. Especially a black female; especially as cold as the world had gotten. May and Ron had decided together before then that it was too chilly to begin with.

Sure, Maybell felt great strides had been made in the community. But for the last several years, she felt as if the world and the struggles her and Mr. Johnson had lived through, had backslid. She remarked to herself in that moment, *It's like a shitty Christian who seems to be a pillar of the community and someone everyone could look up to is suddenly found out to be a thief of the church, the community, or of children. That's what the rights feel like now that we all fought for. It's just another cancer. You feel you got it beat, and they give you your five-year cancer free anniversary, and then it's back again.*

Maybell continued to wait and thought it best to ignore Sunday dress-girl. She didn't want her to come over and get friendly. She wanted no more thoughts of regret that the little girl had stirred up for her regarding never having a child or children. So, while she sat, she again pulled out her receipts that she didn't get to go through during her less-than-private potty time to make sure she wasn't overcharged. Not because she was concerned about every penny, she just didn't like to feel cheated, even accidentally, since her Tootsie Roll days.

While Maybell was lost in thought and in paperwork, she was finally called, but not in the way she had thought she would be. No one else was in the waiting area.

A woman in her forties, overly made up like it was her own high school picture day—big hair and all—came up to the counter from the back where the photos were being taken. Following behind the

47

big hair lady came the Sunday dress-girl and her unruly family. With a final smile toward Maybell, the little girl rounded the corner, then through the shop door, and out of Maybell's head full of regret.

The garish woman called out, "Excuse me, Ms...?"

"Mrs. Johnson," answered Maybell.

"Oh, well, um, Mrs. Johnson, do you have an appointment?"

"An *uh-pernt-ment*?" Maybell questioned.

"Yes, Ma'am, we don't take walk-ins."

"Oh, you don't?" Maybell looked around one shoulder then the next, "You saw me sittin' here over an hour ago, didn't you?"

"Yes, Mrs. Johnson, I did, but I thought you had an appointment."

"Yoooou diiiid? Well, ain't that something. You looked in your uh-pernt-ment book and saw someone listed?"

"No, Ma'am, I didn't, I just assumed..."

"Oh. Oh, I see. You just assumed that a person sitting here would have an uh-pernt-ment, right?"

"Well...well, yes. Yes, I did.

"Now wait, you don't take walk-ins, and having that policy means that you likely have had to turn entire families away who were all dressed up and had waited, no?"

"Yes, Mrs. Johnson, we have," Glamor Gal shot back, clearly irritated.

48

"I see…okay, yes…well, so if you have had to do that before, it must have been awful embarrassin' for everyone involved, right?"

"It might have been for some of them."

"Oh, but not you?" Maybell asked, and it was clear she had caught the tone of Glamor Girl and decided to match it.

"Ma'am, I'm sorry, but we can't take you without an appointment."

"Oh, I understand that fully, dear heart, surely do. Now, let's see," Maybell looked at her watch then back at the attendant, "So, it's 3:45pm, when is the next person or family due to come in?"

"We don't have anyone else on our books," Glamour said with a haughty tone.

"Then will you help me with one more thing, Miss?"

"And what would that be, Mrs. Johnson?"

After smacking her lips, Maybell said as if butter couldn't melt in her mouth, "I'd like to make an Uh-PERT-MENT."

Maybell was glad to see that the photographer was more accommodating once her 4pm uh-pernt-ment rolled around. He was in his fifties and kind. Mr. Billings had been in the photography business for years and was making quick work out of the session, following Maybell's requests for how she would like her headshot taken from the left side. As the photographer positioned his camera, she made sure to make a knowing smile. It's absolutely how she wanted to be portrayed to anyone who saw it in the paper for the few seconds they might scan it, and her life, in obituary form; one that she fully intended to write herself.

"Why are you having this portrait done, Ms. Johnson?"

"Oh, I just felt frisky today!"

"Frisky, huh?"

"Oh, not that frisky."

The two got a nice laugh out of it. The photographer, Mr. Billings, even appeared to be a little flirty with Mrs. Johnson. So much so that when the both of them stopped laughing and Mr. Billings was still looking at Maybell with bedroom eyes, she made it clear right at the end of her laugh that trailed off with a look of, "don't even think about it".

"Oh, you is a youngster to me and even if I did have any intent at all in allowing you to be my suitor, I would work you over so bad I'd bus' yo' ass out the frame, boy." That caused Mr. Billings to change those bedroom eyes of his into ones that now shown embarrassment.

"Now, if you'll excuse me, I need to collect my prints and be on my way. I have another uh-pernt-ment."

"Oh, uh, yes, yes ma'am!"

Back at the front of the store, Glamour Girl decided she would let Mr. Billings complete the sale.

"You have been such a joy, Mr. Billings, thank you so much, these look perfect…and in eight-by-tens, no less. How wonderful."

50

"Yes, Mrs. Johnson, we just got that machine a few months ago so we could print them out digitally right here, so people didn't have to wait."

"Oh my," Maybell said as she stood on her tippy toes to look over Billings' shoulder and locked eyes with Glamour Girl, "that must be to the chagrin of your co-worker, she loves to have people wait for no reason at all."

8

A Snowball's Chance In Hell

One of the few things in life that Maybell still loved was a proper New Orleans sno-ball. In other parts of the south, and in the country, they were more commonly known as a snow cone. The shaved ice that used to be hand-hewn by sno-ball hawkers pushing shopping carts, a block of ice, and the tool of the trade, were replaced by a machine in little five-by-nine buildings on wheels.

The machine that makes the ice fluffy and not "snow cone crunchy" has been around New Orleans, where it was invented, nearly one-hundred years ago. All the flavors one could possibly want are available at little shacks that dot the New Orleans landscape. One could even get a sno-ball that tastes like wedding cake with the fluffy ice on the bottom, soft-serve ice cream in the middle and more "sno" on the top covered in the wedding cake flavor and sweetened condensed milk. However, today, Maybell just wanted the ice cream only. So, she made her way to the ramshackle shack where she always went. She never made small talk, and she didn't go often, so the summertime high school staff didn't know her at all.

Maybell parked in the lot that was topped by a bed of oyster shells that crunched under her tires. Before she even got out of her car, she grumbled at the line that had formed on the porch, down the steps, and out onto the sidewalk. But when Maybell got her mouth all ready for some ice cream, there was little that she allowed to get in her way. Maybell especially wouldn't let anyone get in between her and vanilla soft serve in a cup with the perfectly shaped long handled spoon that fit her mouth just right.

After she waited in line twenty-five to thirty minutes, it was now her turn. The sixteen- to seventeen-year-old young lady slid the glass window opening that was kept closed after every order to help the little window unit air-conditioner keep up with the summertime heat.

"What can I get for you, ma'am?"

"Oh, I just want a large cup of soft-serve vanilla, please," Maybell requested while she started to open the small billfold she had carried with her from the car.

"Oh, we don't have any ice cream today. I mean, we do, but it's only for the sno-balls."

"Excuse me, I'm sorry, I don't understand."

"Our machine is not keeping up with the demand, and we are only using it for the sno-balls people want with ice cream in it."

"So, lemme understand, you do have ice cream. It is soft serve. It is vanilla. But it's only for sno-balls, correct?"

"Yes, ma'am, I'm sorry."

Three adults lined a wooden counter on the back wall with their backs toward the order window that was on their right and the serve window on their left. They didn't turn around because they were busying themselves trying to keep up with the orders already taken by "Little Miss School Child".

Maybell's lip hung like there was a boot in her mouth. "Listen honey, normally I want a sno-ball like a wedding cake, but today I just want soft-serve vanilla in a big ol' cup, ya feel me?"

"Yes, ma'am, I understand. But we had to stop serving it in a cup and just save what we have for the sno-balls."

"I get ya, and you said that, and I can see why you would want to do that but—"

The youngster made the mistake of cutting off ol' Maybell mid-sentence, "Thanks, yeah, sorry about that."

Maybell paused but didn't break her gaze, "—but I jus'…", Maybell changed tactics, "ya know what…how 'bout dis," Maybell's New Orleans dialect started to seep out, "How 'bout you jus' do me the kindness, jus' this once, I mean, I come here often, jus' sneak me a little of that ice cream in a small cup and I'll pay for a large."

The young-un feigned a sad face and slumped her shoulders, "I'm sorry, I can't."

Maybell was taken aback at this point. What business would turn down more money than the product was worth? "I jus' don' un'nastand? I mean you are—"

She did it again, "Yes. Yes, I know it seems weird, but some people are not going to buy a sno-ball at all if they can't get it with ice cream in the middle."

"Yes, I get that. I get the value of what you are sayin'. So how 'bout dis? How 'bout you—"

The young-un turned around to get some adult help but they must not have liked her very much, which was odd, because most of the stands are family owned and run. They were not so much as looking over their shoulders at her. Maybell waited until she turned back around to face her and then she continued, "—how 'bout you do this? Jus' give me the amount of ice cream that you would put in one of those special sno-balls of yours and charge me as if I bought the whole thing? Jus' how 'bout you charge me the whole price for a whole sno-ball with a whole shot of that there soft-serve BUT only put ice cream in the cup?"

But the child had her heals dug in and was on her own because none of the adults in the back wanted any part of ol' Mrs. Maybell.

"I'm sorry, I just can't do that."

Maybell was incredulous. Now they were both in the land of bargaining absurdities and Maybell, knowing that's where she was, made a decision and went for it. She fashioned her hands to create the illusion of manufacturing a sno-ball as she explained, "Okay, how 'bout dis'? How 'bout you take some of that fluffy-ass snow and put it on the bottom," she raised her cupped hands up a few inches and continued, "then, you put ice cream nex', then top it off with more snow and I'll scrape it off and you charge me double, hummm?" Maybell finished her query with her eyes buck wide.

The young girl looked back at the three people right behind her that had yet to turn around. She did this as a last-ditch effort to see if anyone would assist. She knew she was being stubborn and foolish because she had not thought of that type of sale herself. But when the three kept their backs turned and offered no assistance nor acknowledgement, she turned back to Maybell and exclaimed, "No, we ain't doin' that," and the young lady punctuated the remark by slamming the sliding metal and glass window shut.

By this time everyone was looking at Maybell and snickering at the situation. "Da' fuck y'all lookin' at?" Maybell asked the group waiting for their order at the other window. They all looked down, away, or covered their mouth with their hand.

Maybell didn't get beat too often, but she knew when she was. It was the last time she would ever bring her business to that stand. And as fate would have it, they closed shortly after that and never opened again.

9

Mrs. Johnson Visits Her Mr.

Maybell was still smarting from not winning the ice-cream battle royale at the sno-ball stand. She had driven up the road a bit and ambled up to the curb and parked near the wrought iron gate that was the entrance to her city of the dead. Though it was a full city, there was only one citizen there she cared about. It was her late husband of over thirty years, Mr. Ronald Johnson.

Ronald's headstone was weathered but had held up well because Maybell had made sure that it was constructed of marble that cold December fifteen years before. She wanted to do more, but both lived meagerly their entire marriage and were interested more in each other than climbing the corporate ladder at the Folgers coffee plant where they both worked their entire careers. She had worked in bookkeeping and he as a manager on the line.

"Hello, Mr. Johnson," she bellowed. In her head she could hear him say, *Hello, my little Ms. May.* He was the only person in the world, other than her own mother and one other person, that she ever allowed to call her that.

"I went to that raggedy-ass mall today and bought some things…aww, don't fret none, I didn't spend too much. I spent more than I wanted, though. But I must prepare for what's comin' just as much as I must prepare for what goin'. I need to get my affairs in order."

Maybell could just hear him now, again in her head, *what affair you got goin' on? Who is messin' 'round with my girlfriend?* She chuckled at the thought. He had used that joke a few times in their life together. Both knew neither one had a single thing to worry about. She was too curmudgeon for anyone to pine over and he was as loyal as Camille.

"Look, I need to say some things to you, and I don't know if I can get them out. Ronald, I miss you so much, I just can't stand it. Every year that goes by, I keep telling myself it will get easier and every year the world around me becomes darker…*I'm* becoming darker. Darker in thoughts and in a spirit, if I even have one. I'm turning more sullen each year without you here with me to calm my darkness. Camille is getting older but that ol' girl is just as stubborn as I am, so I figure she won't die anytime soon, and I'd be okay with that if I were better. I just want to go back to a time when my life was okay. But Ronald, it won't be better and I'm not okay. I'm not okay and I'm not better without you because you made me better. You made me who I was. You made me who I wanted to be. But that's just about all gone now. It fades more each year like this ol' stone of yours. I just feel like…I dunno…I jus' feel like I don't know if I can do this no more. I don't think I can do it without you. I don't wanna do it no more without you. But I will. I'll keep doin' it…whatever *it* is. Some folk call it livin'. It just feels like it's dying in slow motion to me. And my ol' darkness that you chased away creepin' back up on me. At first, after you passed, it was behind me, and I could keep 'head of it. Now, it walks next to me like an old friend that was never friendly, never nice, and never wanted."

Maybell began to softly weep as she knelt and pushed her index finger into the soaked and soft New Orleans summer ground. "So, like I said, I need to prepare for what's comin' and what's goin'. And I want to leave this with you in case I can't get back here 'cause right now, you can't leave, and I can't stay.

Maybell took Mr. Ronald's wedding band off. She had been wearing it on her thumb since his passing. After she had dug a hole as deeply as she could, she pushed it into the earth that topped his grave, and covered it back up.

"Mr. Johnson, will you marry me...again?"

And in her head, she heard him say clearly, as if he were whispering in her ear, *I do, I would marry you over a thousand lifetimes, my sweet May.*

10

Who Dat?

Maybell was exhausted as she was greeted by Camille who was as hungry as Maybell was tired, "Punkin', I'm sorry I lef' you 'lone so damned long. I ran into all kinds of hassle and now I'm wore plum slap. Lemme getcha something to eat, ol' girl."

The Widow Johnson poured dried chow in Camille's bowl. Maybell then took out a second bowl and opened a can of wet food as a treat to her last love for having left her alone all day. Once done, she went to her bedroom with her bags from the day's shopping.

"Gotdayum that is some stank, Camille," Maybell exclaimed as she walked into her bedroom. Camille may be breaking the rules and sleeping in May's marital bed all day, but she would never potty there, however, there was plenty in her cage. "You been eatin' opossum when I ain't home, girl? Ooo lawd I'mma have to clean that shit up before I go to bed. Stank be all loud! How you want momma to sleep with all that goin' on?" Camille never looked up from her bowl and Maybell was busying herself by getting changed

60

as she kidded her sweetheart, "I know everyone void stank but I mean, dayum!"

On the few occasions when Maybell would leave the house long enough for her not to be able to let Camille out back to run around and "do her business", she would just make sure the tray in the bottom of the kennel was freshly lined. Although there were blankets and old quilts, they were always around the perimeter of the center and Camille would never potty on them. Though, she was starting to miss the center a little and Maybell thought each of the last few times she cleaned, it was because her mutt was getting old. Still, it was a rare event that she left Camille in the house long enough that she wouldn't wait to go outside.

Maybell was hungry, she hadn't gotten to eat her ice cream and was still pissy about getting beat in a game of mind checkers by the young lady at the sno-ball stand. She decided she needed to settle down that sweet tooth. After carefully hanging up her new dress, belt, and placing the hat in an old hat box that had a few worn ones, including Mr. Johnson's favorite bolo with a little feather in it, she got back into her beloved stretchy pants and another drab blouse. Maybell went into the adjoining kitchen where Camille had just finished gorging herself and couldn't walk much. When Maybell opened the cupboard, Camille took a new interest in what was coming out next—an unopened package of Oreos. Maybell next took some milk from the fridge and off both of them went into the living room to see what the 5:30 national news had in the way of world horrors. Maybell would then flip around the channels and wait for a good ol' fashioned Dateline. She hoped Keith Morrison was the man of the hour because he was her favorite. He was always over the top, always well delivered, and he was always assigned the best murder mysteries.

Maybell flew her bare feet up on the Lay-Z-Boy footrest with the flick of the bar on the left-hand side of the base after sitting the milk down on a TV tray that was always near and cookies on her stomach. Using the remote, she kicked on the television and tried to get after those cookies.

Maybell worked on the packaging slowly at first because she was distracted by the top stories. Then she quickened her pace because she was having little success in how she was pinching the front of the bag that sealed the tray. She kept working at it carefully because, if experience had taught her anything, it was that if she pulled too hard and too quick it was all over, and Camille would get half a sleeve of cookies before Maybell could even get out of the chair.

"Man, they don't want you to get in these," Maybell fussed as she finally tore the bag open. Though she lost none from the tray inside, she still ripped the bag in a way that it was not going to seal properly. She pulled two out and one of them went right to Camille who knew this drill, and she knew she was only going to get three. "Now, don't you eat that one too fast, girl. You know they say chocolate can kill dogs. Sho' didn't kill yo' ass when you ate that whole box of Ding-Dongs I lef' out that time," Maybell remembered aloud, "Man, I'm still missin' dem Ding-Dongs." With that, she dropped another cookie for the mutt and settled into her news and treats as she dipped one after the other into milk for herself.

It was twenty cookies and four hours later when she heard the noise. It wasn't loud, nor was it discernible to Maybell as to what it was. It was the kind of sound that one would know was loud at its central location but too far away to guess what caused it; the kind of noise that isn't close enough to hurt you but close enough to pique your interest. Camille had raised her head and one ear toward the tv which shared a wall with the outside world.

Maybell's back was to the window, so she turned and looked over her shoulder to peer through it. She only found that the curtains were pulled closed and it was now dark enough to make it difficult to see anything through them. She and Camille, both knew that wasn't where the sound came from, anyway. It was like a muffled shriek, and it was short. Maybell pushed down on the footrest of her chair and quickly got to her feet. Camille followed but didn't walk in front of her master. Mrs. Johnson made her way to the front door, opened it slowly, and peered out. She saw nothing but what looked to be a rental car outside. It had a little green and white sticker on the back that that read *Enterprise*. She peered out further to find there was no sound at all other than the crickets. The wave of New Orleans night heat drove her back inside, though she wasn't satisfied the sound was nothing to be concerned about.

As Maybell shut the door, Camille let out a little pre-bark to let her master know that she wasn't satisfied either and that she intended to stay alert. "What chew gonna do, Cammy? You ain't gone do shit. But I trust ya. Keep both dem floppy ears straight up and listenin'," Maybell half whispered. The two went back to watching another crime show but Camille kept her head up and one ear at the ready for five full minutes until she settled back on her paws.

The 10pm top stories were nothing exciting. New Orleans was serious about their news and had broadcasts at Five, six, and 10pm. That's why so many of their newscasters ended up on the national stage; Hoda Kotb being one of several. There wasn't anything new on the news and the weather was too far away to care about staying up to see. Maybell decided it was time for bed after such a trying day.

"Com'on girl, it's time," Maybell said with a chirp and Camille hopped to her feet, beat her master to the bedroom, and jumped on the bed. "You are clear ouch yo' mind, girl. How many years we gotta go through this? You get in that cage and get in there now," Maybell gave her time and grace to slowly get off the bed. She was busy, anyway, putting on her P-jams and a bathrobe because she was still going to sit in front of her vanity and take off that make-up she had on all day. As she began to use the half-dried makeup remover sheet, both ladies heard another sound.

There was a mop-headed man of slight build in his mid-thirties, wearing blue jeans and a black shirt, who had crept around the side of Maybell's house. There was a wooden screen door just before the solid wood door. It was flimsy and made a creaking sound when he opened it. Without hesitation, he smashed a pane of glass, reached in the little opening, and unlocked the dead bolt. Once inside, it was dark, and his eyes need to adjust because he had looked up at the light that was on the right side of the doorway leading into the kitchen. Once his eyes had adjusted, he saw more than he ever thought he would that night.

Camille was just sitting there, three feet from the opening. The pretend burglar didn't even see her for a few seconds as he crept all the way in. Once he noticed her, he stopped dead in his tracks and Cammy didn't move an inch.

A voice from his left was low and deliberate, "Oh, don't you worry 'bout her none. She would show you where the silverware was if I had any, but I don't," Maybell said as she moved out of the shadows and into the light that was showing through the door that was still open. Both the intruder's feet were past the threshold. He started to pull one back to place it on the step behind him and slowly creep out.

"Umm umm, no you don't," Maybell said as calm and as low as if she were talking to a toddler who was about to break a rule while looking dead in their parent's eyes. "See, you done fucked up, now. Both your feet are in my house. If I decided to shoot you dead, I'm well within my rights." It was then that he saw the snub-nosed .38 in Maybell's hand. It was Mr. Johnson's revolver that he had never once fired other than to teach May how to do so.

"And if you try and turn and act like I shot you in the back I have two things going for me: if you flinch, I'm still going to be fast enough to get ya from the front, you ol' buzzard, and if I ain't and I get you in the back, what DA is gone charge a little ol' lady who was minding her own business and keeping her house and puppy safe? Either way, you dead and I'm free. Now, why don't you come in here real nice and slow like and then we decide what to do with ya."

"Look, ma'am, I'm sorry, I got the wrong house," the man said with his palms up and arms raised halfway.

"You sure as hell did. Now, come on in and set a spell while we figure this little misunderstandin' out."

"I'm just gonna back out real slow," but as he said that he lunged for Maybell. With her other hand that didn't have a gun in it, Maybell swung with all her might and hit Mr. Burglar over the head with an eight-inch cast iron skillet. He hit the floor with a solid thud and laid motionless. Camille let out one sharp bark as if she were saying, *That's right, that's what you get!*

11

Captive Audience

The man awoke with a headache worse than any hangover he had ever had, and he had experienced many, but it was usually from being in bars and not behind them. The bars he was used to being in were much larger. He was only able to open his right eye, but even with one eye open, he could tell he was in a cage that was only two and a half or three feet wide and maybe four feet long.

Every slight movement made a creaking sound, and the stench of piss and shit made his head hurt even worse than it would have with only the knot the skillet had left on his skull. Surveying his cage that contained his six-foot frame and the room that it was in, left him wondering how he even ended up there. His head was still fuzzy about the event. That's when he saw Maybell, sitting on the bed, the gun in her lap, and his wallet open in her hands like a small new testament Bible. She heard the creaking in the cage and knew he was starting to come-to.

"Well, goot evening, sleepy head. How's that big ol' knot Bertha give ya?"

"Ms. Bertha, I don't know what you hit me with," his voice creaked as he spoke, "but I—"

"It's Mrs. Maybell Johnson. You can call me Mrs. Johnson. Bertha is the name of the skillet I hit you with. It was my grandmother's. Well-seasoned, too. Makes the best cornbread you ever had. Slides right out like goose shit though a tin horn."

"Mrs. Johnson, I'm real sorry, but I ain't never had a headache like this in my life. You got some aspirin or Tylenol?"

"Aspirin? Tylenol? That shit don't work! I got some ibuprofen I picked up fo' my hip a while back. I'll go get ya some. But, if while I'm gone, I hear that cage creak a lick, Imma come in here and leave you with more holes than you was born with."

"Okay, yes. Yes. Deal, Mrs. uhh."

"Mrs…John-Son."

"Yes, Mrs. Johnson. I can't move, anyway."

Maybell looked at him side eyed as she slowly stood up from her bed and Camille followed her into the bathroom. As he looked around with the one eye he could open while lying in a fetal position and not moving any other muscles, he noticed there was a cartoonishly large brass padlock on the cage he was in. The cage that held him was in the corner of an unkempt bedroom in the back of the shotgun house. There was a vanity on the other side of the room against the same wall his cage was on. He could hear Mrs. Johnson rifling around in the bathroom that was off the hallway from the bedroom. He heard the sink turn on and a cup being filled.

Maybell returned and commanded, "Turn yo' head, open yo' mowf, and hope these pills fall in that hole in your face." As she made her demand she held the gun out toward him. Groaning, he turned his head, opened his mouth, and hoped for the best. Maybell dropped the pills through the larger than mesh sized opening, and three of the four caplets found their mark.

"Oh, it must be yo' lucky day. Now, keep that face open." She brought the water cup up to the same spot and tipped it slowly at first then full tilt. The water hit his mouth, face, and entire side of his neck, "I always wondered what it would be like to waterboard somebody," Maybell said as she plopped the cup on top of the cage and calmly walked back to the edge of her bed. "Now, let's see who my first and only victim is."

Mrs. Johnson sat the gun in her lap and reopened his wallet, "Joseph Lee Caruso?" Maybell though for a moment and looked up at the man in the cage whose name she now read again because she had already read it when he was out cold.

"Naw, you ain't gonna be no 'Joseph' while you are a guest in my home. You gonna be a 'Joey'. A Joseph wouldn't have been bus' in the head and put in no dog cage by me. That's nothin' more than a 'Joey'," Maybell mocked.

"Ma'am, uh, Mrs. Johnson, you can call me anything you want if you just let me go," Joseph suppressed his look of surprise when Maybell mentioned his real name and not the one on the bogus driver's license that was much easier to find in the front of his wallet.

"Let you go? You fuckin' kiddin' me? No indeed not, not yet anyway. Me and Camille ain't come to no conclusion what we gone

69

do with chew yet," Maybell went back to looking through his wallet. "Lubbock Texas, huh? Humm, now, what would a man from Lubbock be doing here in New Orleans East, and in a rented car, no less?"

"How do you know that isn't a fake driver's license?"

"Because the one that has 'Joseph Lee Caruso' printed on it was hidden. The other one with that bogus name on it wasn't. You might think I'm some ignant ol' lady, but I ain't. If there are two of the same things and one is hidden and one ain't, then that means the one that is all tucked away is the person's real identity. Plus, it matched all but one of the credit and ATM cards you got in here…except for one shiny new one. Probably the one you been using to get here. For what reason, I don't know…YET…but that's a problem for another day. So, what's it gonna be, Joey? Why are you here other than up to no good?"

"I'm just trying to get me a few bucks or some shit to fence."

Maybell picked up her gun and pointed it at Joey, "DON'T YOU DARE SWEAR IN MY MOTHA' FUCKIN' HOUSE!"

"I'm sorry. Yes, yes Mrs. Johnson. I'm sorry. I'm just looking for some money or drugs."

"You ain't no drug addict. If you was, you would have asked for something stronger than aspirin and you wouldn't have been wearing them expensive-ass boots," Maybell pointed with the nose of the revolver over to his boots that had been removed and tossed in the corner, "and you wouldn't have those expensive-ass jeans you wearin', neither."

"I'm tellin' you the truth, I promise."

70

"That's not even close to the truth, Joey," as she tossed his wallet on top of the cage. It hung half open and one of the halves had slid in-between the cage bars and dangled there. Joey retrieved it and slid it into his back pocket. It was in that moment that he slowly slid his right hand, that he was partially laying on, toward his pocket where his buck knife was. But this time, it wasn't.

"Oh, you lookin' fo' this, Joey?" Maybell asked as she held out the lock blade. She sat down her firearm and opened the knife. It was caked with dried blood. "Uh oh, is this blood?"

"It's not what it looks like."

"Oh, you left Texas to deer hunt in the Sportsman's Paradise when it ain't even huntin' season? You may be here to hunt, but it ain't fo' no deer and it ain't fo' no sport."

Joey just laid his head down to let the pain go away. All of it—on his head as well as in it.

"Humph, that's what I thought. Wait, you kill ol' Gadfly next door? That's what that noise was earlier? Oh, you may have made my day."

Joey just slowly looked over and made a face like he smelled something bad.

"What? Too soon?" Maybell quipped.

"I just wouldn't expect a lady to be that cavalier about thinking that someone killed her neighbor."

"Ooooh, 'cavalier'. Cammy, we got us an educated killer in yo' cage. Look, bottom line is I ain't no lady and the next-door bitch talked too much."

71

"I'll make sure I don't make the same mistake."

"You'd do well not to. I may not have a final plan for you yet, but I do plan on one thing."

"What's that?" Joey asked, a little intrigued and very concerned.

"I got me a captive audience. And I got some shit I wanna say. And I don't take kindly to being interrupted."

12

Cornbread, Ham, and Monologues

Joey must have passed out and slept through the rest of the night because when he opened his eye, there was too much sunlight and the smell of something cooking. It sounded like a radio was on down the hall and something sizzling. He could hear it was music, then some talking, then more music. However, he couldn't make out the songs, nor the speeches of the D.J.

Maybell rounded the corner of the door and looked down into the cage, "Well, goot mornin', Joey. You sleep well?"

"I'm sorry Mrs. Johnson but not really."

"I bet not. Not with that big bump on yo' noggin'."

Joey slowly reached up and felt his head with his hand for the first time. It was like someone had cut a golf ball in half and shoved it under his scalp.

"Yeah, that's what ya git from bustin' in some poor ol' lady's house," Maybell let out a short snort of a laugh. "Hey, you want 'nother couple of dem ibuprofen's?"

"Yes Mrs. Johnson. Please, if you wouldn't mind."

"Oh, I don't mind at all, Joey. Surely don't."

She walked over, got the cup off the top of the cage, and completed the same task as the night before. Although, this time she let him hold out his hand to catch the pills, but she poured the water just the same. She finished the ghoulish task by putting the cup back on the top of her captive's cell.

"You want some cornbread and ham steak? Boy, I sure do love me some cornbread. I made it in the same skillet I bus' yo' head with." Her darkness had never been so entertained nor in command, or maybe it was in control. "It's just too late fo' grits an' eggs," she said.

"Yes ma'am, I am hungry but I need to use the bathroom."

"Not my bathroom you don't. You ain't comin' outta that cage. You use it right where you sit. If it's good enough for Camille, it's most certainly good enough for yo' butter head-ass." Maybell thought for a moment, "Hey, maybe I should call you 'ol' Pissy Pants'."

"Mrs. Johnson, please, can you just—"

Maybell had been looking at the clock as "Pissy Pants" had been starting his sentence.

"Oh, hold that thought, it's time to take the cornbread out *and* it's time for my update!" Maybell looked over and softly said, "I'll jus' give you some privacy, Mr. Joey Pissy Pants while I check on some things." She slowly and quietly closed the door while looking at Joey and flashing a devilish grin.

74

Joey had no idea what her "update" was, who it was from, nor what it was about—at that point nothing mattered to him. Joey pissed himself and sat in the dog's filth, as well as his own. He could hear the TV on now and the radio had been turned off. Regardless, he couldn't hear anything that was being said, it was simply a low mumbling, but it did sound like a newscast in cadence. Soon, the radio was back on. The door opened slowly, and Maybell peeked in, "All done, pissy pants?"

He just nodded his head "yes".

"Wonderful! Now, let's eat. The update say we good fo' now."

"Good? Good how?"

"Oh, nothing of any concern of yours. Jus' a lil ol' update about things goin' on in the world," she finished as she disappeared around the corner and back into the kitchen.

The radio was turned up loud enough now with the door open that he could tell it was the band *Earth, Wind, and Fire*, but didn't remember the name of the song that was being played. It was still a bit much for his, now partially numbed, headache.

Maybell came around the corner again, still in her pink house coat, a plate in each hand, and dancing with a silly smile on her face and eyes closed. "Man, those were the days, when music was music, ya feel me?"

Joey didn't answer but tried to slowly sit up and having no idea how he was going to get the ham steak and cornbread through those cage bars.

Maybell sat both plates on the bed and warned Camille, who had followed her everywhere she went, not to go anywhere near those plates. She didn't and instead followed Maybell back to the kitchen. Joey could hear dog food filling a bowl, the bag getting plopped back on the floor, the fridge opening, and then cups being filled with soda.

Maybell returned, a cup in each hand, still dancing to EW&F. After setting both cups on her bedside table, she laid a paper plate near the cage and a plastic fork with all but one tine busted off. The ham steak was cut up into tiny squares, but not the cornbread that was topped with a huge chunk of melting butter. She sashayed back over to the edge of her bed, bopping along to the tune that was ending. Then the announcer came on before the song had even stopped playing.

"Gotdaym it! I can't STAND those D.J.'s"

In his mind, Joey started to work his way out of that cage, "Why?" he asked. Not because he cared, but because in his line of work, other people had tried doing the same thing to him. His victims would attempt to get him to let his guard down. It never worked but he did find himself getting a little soft sometimes depending on how good they were, though he would still kill them, anyway. He'd let them live just a little longer before he watched the hope leave their face, their eyes, their soul.

He was hopeful, though, regarding his own plight. He had already come to believe that Mrs. Johnson was unhinged, but that she may be more reasonable than he would be if given the same circumstances. She could let him go; she didn't have a reason to kill him. If she would have, had she made her mind up to do so, it would have happened the night before rather than knocking him unconscious, at least that's what made sense to him. He slid two pincher fingers through a slit in the cage and picked up the near tine-less fork, stabbed a piece of ham, and tried to work it through the skinny bars of the makeshift cell.

"Why? What chew mean, 'why'?" Maybell asked after having already bit into a piece of the sweet cornmeal cake and started to answer with her whole mouth full, "Look, those butt nuggets are simply frustrated musicians. I can't think what in the world makes them feel so special. I mean, honestly, I DO know what they think! They think they are part of the band," Maybell made a motion like she was strumming a guitar, flinging cornbread crumbs on the bed and to the floor. "It ain't even as difficult as it was in the seventies when they had to put a record on a platter and make sure that it mixed right into the next song. Now they got those compact discs or some shit, and it's all computerized. But that ain't even the part that bugs me the most. It's all that fuckin' yappin' they do. Like they on stage, tellin' these lame-ass jokes. I ain't laughed once at shit a D.J. said in my whole life. And don't even get me started with the morning shows where all they do is fuckin' talk. Oh lawd, I just want to see them all get fired. I heard about that satellite radio they came out with. I was in a cab and the driver started bragging about it, then a commercial came on promoting the fuckin' product we was listenin' to. I mean, how dim! If you can hear the commercial, you must already have a subscription, right? I mean, I didn't, but you get my pernt. 'All music. All the time' they said. 'Commercial free' they said. Before long, they start sneaking in the D.J.'s, I jus' knew they would. A year later, after I was in that cab, I was in a little store to get my hair supplies and sure 'nuff, there they was, D.J.'s talking over, above, and about the music they were playing. The history of it, what they was gone play the next hour, and some goddamned anecdote-y quip about when they met Led Zeppelin thirty years ago and how they never forgot it."

Maybell took another bite of cornbread like the story wouldn't be as good unless her mouth was totally full.

"Me and Mr. Johnson loved us some Led Zeppelin, that's my dead husband, anyway, give me a fuckin' break. Who the shit called up and said, 'hey, ya know what, Imma cancel my subscription unless you give us the D.J.'s like the radio stations that we can listen to for free. OH, and slap some commercials in there while you at it? WHO SAID THAT? NOBODY, THAT'S WHO!"

Maybell stabbed a big piece of ham with her fork and then started to wave in the air in a circular motion.

"No, what they needed a way to keep their tagline, 'commercial free music'. So, whadda they do? They hire D.J.'s to hawk stuff. The D.J.'s became the commercials. Now they tellin' you products they use, what websites to go to, where the bands will be, and when they gonna be there. Like Imma fly to fuckin' Chicago to see, well, CHICAGO! Then the nerve to give the listener a five-minute backstory about how they used to be called The Chicago Transit Authority! I DON'T GIVE TWO BALLS OF GOAT SHIT WHAT THEY WAS CALLED AND I ALREADY KNEW THAT BECAUSE IF I'M LISTENING TO CHICAGO ON THEIR BRAND OF 70'S STATION IT MEAN THAT I PROBABLY LIVED DURING THAT TIME AND SAW THAT FUCKIN' PRINTED ON AN ALBUM COVER BEFORE I PULLED THE RECORD OUTTA THE SLEEVE, TOSSED THAT BITCH ON THE PLATTER, PINCHED THE ARM, DROPPED THE

NEEDLE, AND PLAYED WHAT I WANTED TO HEAR! And I can tell ya this, Joey, it weren't no D.J. I wanted to hear; it's the tunes. It's 'bout the music."

Maybell took a bit of the ham from the fork she had been waving around and then fed some to Cammy who was watching her very animated master the whole time she monologued.

"Then they got the nerve to charge you for the privilege," Maybell paused only long enough to chew and look off into the distance as Joey managed to get only the second of two ham cubes through the bars as she continued, "Yeah, so I hate D.J.'s. Especially the ones who went on to get their own radio shows like some of the locals here in the city on the free radio. They have whole stations where they used to play music and now they act like they some type of Jerry Springer-ass shit. The call-in shows, ya know. Joey, I dunno about what shit they got in Texas, but here they got a whole gaggle of dem' doofuses on a station. And it's a station that used to play nothing but music. Some of 'em used to be D.J.'s and some used to be TV sportscasters or some shit. Hell, even some actor, who I understand ain't half bad but only done some stage plays and bit parts in movies, he even be there. Just yip yappin' and acting like they have an opinion that matters because they got a microphone in front of their big fat face. Lawd, then they go and cut off the people who have something real to say and they let the ones who you want to shoot in the back of the head just keep on talkin'. Real stupid rascals, too," Maybell went on to mock in a nasally voice, "'That's what's wrong with the world today, I think they just need to make weed legal and they just need to tax the corporations and they blah blah blah'! Yeah, tax the corporations and they pass it right on to the consuma'! That means we just pay a higher price. Fuck faces! Give someone a Mr. Microphone and all the sudden they have all the answers to the world's problems," Maybell looked over at Joey in the cage. "Hey, so how's that ham?"

"Ummm, humm, Mrs. Johnson," Pissy Pants said through a forced smile. It wasn't like he was going to say anything else. But Joey never liked ham, his cornbread was all broken up as he tried to get it through the bars on the one tined fork, and he knew, without a doubt, he needed to get something to pick that lock. Mrs. Johnson was going to either kill him dead or make him wish he was.

13

Columbo

Maybell picked up her plate along with Joey's half-eaten one and brought them into the kitchen. "Oh, I almost forgot to give you some drink. But I have to admit, I feel jus' a little bad about waterboarding you. Well, not really, but it's messy business. I have an idea!"

Maybell came back from the kitchen with nothing in her hands, so Joey wasn't sure he liked whatever idea she had. She walked past his cage with Cammy in tow until she reached the back door of the bedroom that led outside.

"Now, Imma open this door, and you bet not make a peep, you hear me?"

"Yes, ma'am."

"Camille, you stay here," she finished as she looked over at Joey, "And don't you even think about trying to call her over to you for no reason at all, ya feel me?"

"I feel ya, Mrs. Johnson."

Maybell opened the back door and looked around before stepping out, "Man, I almost feel like a freed slave now that Gadfly is sitting over there in her own rot. Not having to worry about her trying to talk to me is better than vanilla soft-serve," and with that, she shut the door and walked to the shed.

Joey looked around the room again while Camille made soft whines for her love to return. He looked toward Maybell's bedside table, where a few medicine bottles and a cup next to an eighty's style lamp stood. Used crumpled up tissues were scattered on the surface around the lamp and a ragged copy of *Helter Skelter* completed the whole affair. On the bed, was a quilt that was old and worn. A chest of drawers was on the left side of the door Maybell had just gone out of. He was searching for a key to the big brass lock and the keys to his rental car, but knew that would be a near impossibility to get to or even find. He could hear faint rattling around in what he figured was the garage that was at the end of the driveway on the right of the house if one were facing the front door from the street.

"Camille," he called to the mutt and didn't even know why. After thinking about it for a moment he came to the conclusion that there may be a time when the dog would be of some use. Like in *Silence Of The Lambs* where he could use her love for the ol' bitch against her or maybe he could use Camille to retrieve something. Then, even as bad as the situation he was in was, he had to laugh to himself because it wasn't like *Pirates of the Caribbean*. He had only been to Disney once, but he remembered the guys that are in the jail, and the dog had the key, and they were whistling to him. Camille had no key, and he was risking his life to have that dog come anywhere near that cage. When he called, she didn't move, anyway.

Maybell's face appeared in the window. She tapped on the glass with the head of a short handle axe. Before she opened the door, she asked through the window with a muffled voice, "Did you just call my dog?"

Joey slowly nodded his head, 'yes'.

Maybell gently opened the door and walked in with the axe, headfirst. "She ain't gone listen to you, and she ain't gone help you none. I got what will help you, anyway," she noted as she shook the axe in his direction. His eye opened wider than it had since he first saw the gun in her hand the night before. Even his swollen eye cracked open slightly.

Maybell looked at the axe and back at Joey, "Oh this? Na. We don't need this, not yet anyway, but we shall see. You call my dog again and then we'll know fo' sho'. Nope, I got something else fo' you."

Maybell walked past the cage and Cammy followed. Joey heard the sink running and Maybell came back with a red funnel; she was drying it with a dirty looking hand towel. When she had finished, she plopped it through the top of the cage.

"Mr. Johnson used to use this to fill the lawn mower. I have a neighbor boy mow my lawn now. He's an alright kid. I thought you was him, though, when you first busted in. You never know what kind of people folk really are. He might be a good kid, but people get desperate," Maybell said as she turned and retrieved the cup of

Coke from her bedside table. "Okay, little lamb. Put yo' mowf on the spigot. Go on, do it, if you want some of this here refreshment."

Joey did as instructed, and she began to pour while he drank.

"Jus' look at cha. Like a hamsta' in some little kid's room." She quit pouring and sat back on the bed. Joseph could still taste the left-over fuel on his lips from the funnel.

Maybell broke the silence, "You know why Columbo was one of the best shows on television?"

"I never watched it. I mean, I know about it, I just never watched an episode."

"Oh, you missed a good one there. They still run 'em on a cable channel or two. You know, the ones where they show the classics. Me and the Mr. used to watch it when it was popular in the seventies. Even some of the episodes from the nineties was good. Anyway, Mr. Johnson used to read in here while I watched 'Columbo' out in the front room, at least until he got hooked. See, it's a great design how they used to tell the stories. The first third or fourth of each episode would be showing how the killer did it. The rest of the show was Columbo investigatin', houndin', showin' up wherever the killer was and asking questions. Mr. Johnson came into the living room one night and jus' flat out asked me, 'May, why you watch that show? You already know who the killer is'. I told him the same thing Imma tell you."

Maybell looked over and at her captive audience, "It's seeing how he gone catch 'em, Joey," Mrs. Johnson finished by ceremoniously pulling some paper from her housecoat. "See, what made me think of that was I went out to your rental car after you passed out and I found this paypa, and a few other things."

Maybell unfolded the paper while talking in a "peek-a-boo" tone to Joey, "Where's Gadfly? Where is she?" Maybell held up the paper quickly, "THERE SHE IS!"

Joey just stared at the paper because he knew it had Gadfly's name, address, and phone number on it.

"So, ya see, you *were* here for Gadfly, and I want to figure out why. So, I got to thinkin' 'bout the fact that she was just braggin' 'bout selling off her life insurance policy to the company that has those stupid commercials. God, I hate commercials," Maybell trailed off looking at the ceiling. "Well, anyway, here she is, in your car, and it's most likely her blood on your knife. My information wasn't anywhere near your car. And my address wasn't, neither. Then I was thinkin', 'Man, if dem kids was hopin' to cash in on that life insurance, they were going to be all sad and sorry to find out that she already sold the policy'. I also was thinkin', 'if they don't like her half as much as I don't'…well, didn't, you know, all past tense an' shit, they just might hire someone to do her sorry-ass in. But I wondered if she told any of them that she sold her shit off. Or maybe that's why they got you to do her in before she could go further and get one of those reverse mortgages for the same reason she sold her insurance policy. She get the payout now. Then, when she kicks the bucket, the bank or company or whatever gets the rest of her shit. I know fo' a fact that house is paid off, 'cause she couldn't wait to brag about it years ago. What I don't quite get is why you wouldn't make it look like an accident. Those insurance underwriters go to diggn' 'round when somethin' looks suspicious, so they don't have to pay out if they find somethin'. Why use a knife? Don't tell me that bitch saw you and fought back before you could make it look like an accedent. Probably started howlin' and caterwaulin' and you needed to just end it."

Joey sat still, didn't say a word, and just looked into Maybell's eyes because he didn't want to flinch. If he did live after giving away too much, the people who hired him would likely hire someone to kill him just the same. *Maybell may be a bit batty, but she isn't stupid*, he thought, *She'll sell me down the river with anything I reveal to her*.

It was at that moment that Joey "Pissy Pants" realized that what he needed in order to free himself from that cage wasn't on the outside of it.

It was in it.

14

In Front, Behind, And Beneath

"Welp, I suppose we got us a little bit of a Scooby-Doo mystery. My guess is I'll pull the ol' mask off you yet. I ain't got no computer and I ain't got no internet and I ain't gonna go to the lie-bury to look up shit about you or anything else. I guess I'll jus' have to think of some creative ways to make you talk."

"You don't need to be creative, I told you—"

"You tol' me some bullshit, Joey. I ain't 'bout no bullshit!"

"You can believe me or not."

"Well thank ya very much fo' yo' per-mish-on, butterhead. Imma fig-ya this out my-own-self." Maybell looked at the clock on her vanity, it was turned where Joey couldn't see it, but she could. "Oh, it's just 'bout that time." Maybell lifted off the bed and as she started toward the bedroom doorway, she bent over the cage. "Now, you don't go nowhere," and left the room, shutting the door behind her.

Caruso waited a few seconds until he could hear the television kick on. He looked at the shadow in front of him that the sun cast on the floor through the back door window. The panes' shadows made it so he would be able to tell when some of these timed "updates" that Maybell seemed so keen on catching were to occur and he mentally filed that away.

He put his thumb on his belt buckle. It was a regular style buckle that had a tine just small enough that with a little luck he had an idea of what to do with it. It was flat on the tip and it just might work, but for him to know, he had to take some risks.

Leaning his back on the part of the cage that was against the wall, Joseph felt along the edge from the bottom where it met the metal floor. The cage was designed so that it sat atop four-inch stilts and under it were two trays to catch any filth that a dog might leave behind. The floor itself only had small gaps in it so a dog wouldn't get their paws caught in between the slats of metal. Large amounts of filth wouldn't fall through, not solid turds, anyway. However, that wasn't Joey's concern, he was feeling for where the cage was screwed together. He was so elated that he could hardly contain his emotion when he felt the first screw head where the back of the cage was connected to the frame. He didn't have time to remove his belt to see if that flat-headed tine was small enough to fit into the slot. It wasn't an old enough cage to have flathead screws; they were the Phillips head type. By his guesstimation alone, he felt he had a ghost of a chance of putting in that tine and get enough torque to turn the screw. His next problem was that the back of the cage was only an inch or so from the wall. It might create great cover, but unless he could push that cage at least a few more inches away from the wall, he wouldn't be able to get that belt buckle at the right angle. That was a problem for another time.

Joey continued to feel his way up the back corner of his box and found that the second screw was near the top. He now estimated that the other side must only have two screws, as well. Only four screws held the entire back of the cage to the frame. Joey thought that if he could get the privacy and the time, he would really only need to get two screws out and he could kick the back off that fucker and be on his merry way. He felt his belt buckle with one hand while, with the other, he continued running his finger back down to the bottom screw. Maybe he was feeling too hopeful or too desperate, but he was almost sure he could accomplish the task. The only problem now was simply about not getting caught. The television went off and he put his hands out to his sides and sat up slightly. Maybell opened the door.

"There's still hope for you yet," she said with a smile. "Imma take me a hot shower."

"Alrighty," Joey said back with a real smile this time.

"Oh, you got that brain of yours cookin', Joey. I like that. I like a challenge. Do you?"

"I've had enough challenges to last a lifetime, already. I think I'll just sit in my own filth and your dog shit until you decide what to do with me and all those updates you keep worrying yourself with."

"Oh, ain't no worries here. Not fo' me, anyway. We'll both know soon enough if there are any worries and how much of it will go 'round. You know what they say, 'time will tell'," Maybell said as she disappeared from the door, leaving it open.

Once entering the bathroom that shared a wall with her bedroom and the Joey cage, she slid out of her slippers. She left the bathroom door open, placed her firearm on the tank of the toilet, and turned on the shower. She pulled the shower certain open and then closed it again without getting in. Joey was listening for that shower curtain to close, and she knew he would be.

Maybell crept to the door of the bathroom and waited. She was interested in what ol' Joey Pissy Pants had going on in that busted brain of his. She crept further toward the bedroom door that wasn't but two feet from the bathroom. Maybell peered slowly around the corner, and what she saw was Joseph Caruso already staring at her. It was one of the few times in her life when she got the chills.

Joey had kept still because he had not been convinced she had gotten into that shower. This was gamesmanship and he didn't want to make Maybell mad because she still had the upper hand. But he was starting not to care if he lived nor died, just as long as he did so by trying to get free.

"You left the water running," Joey said.

Maybell eased back out of the doorway as she said nothing, and the expression on her face never changed; neither did her gaze. That gave Pissy Pants just as much of a chill as he had given her. Neither knew to what extent they were both starting to respect their adversary. But she held all the cards for now, including one important card that Mr. Johnson had once owned since he was a child.

However, there was a third adversary looming, and she was becoming more and more angry by the hour. This angry foe was

going to set both Maybell and Joseph free from their deadlock and
their lives.

15

Rectal Exam

After Maybell's shower, Joey could hear her fussing with something in the kitchen. When she reentered the room, Joey looked up, and both acted like nothing had happened a half-hour earlier. She was wrapped in her housecoat, and her feet were covered in slippers. Maybell had a bag of popcorn that appeared to be half empty and two cups of Coke. She sat the sodas down and went over to the cage.

"Cup ya hands."

Joey did as he was instructed, and Camille looked on while licking her chops. The stench in the cage had gone a long way to help keep Joey's hunger down, but he figured since he wanted to stay alive and she was willing to keep him that way, for now, he might as well take whatever food she offered. Maybell shook the bag over the top of the cage and watched it rain down the white cheddar puffs of popped corn on his head; a few fell in his hands. She went to her bed and sat where she normally would when she wanted to do more talking. This time, however, she slid back against the headboard.

"Ya' know, while I was in the shower I was thinking you really did me a kindness by getting rid of ol' Gadfly. She was such an irritant, like a shitty Pampa'—"

"I didn't get rid of no—"

"Shut up, Joey, I'm tryin' to give thanks…lyin'-ass. Anyway, I can go get my mornin' paypa in peace now."

"What that ol' lady ever do to you?"

"Humph, what she ever done YOU? And how would you know she was old 'less you seen her?"

Joey just looked down at the last piece of corn and tossed it in his mouth and Maybell didn't wait for an answer.

"Like I said, every time I went out there, she went to wavin' and hollerin' to get my attention to tell me some bullshit about this and that. Usually, it was 'bout some sort of ailment or financial windfall," Maybell looked over at Joey, "She was one of those people."

"You're talking about her in the past-tense, like you know she's dead. Why don't you go over there and take a gander?"

"First of all, my fingerprints were all over your knife before I wiped it down, and I jus' know that was her blood on it. Second of all, you ain't gonna get me over there and leave evidence that implicates me in no crime. Third, the less time I give you alone, the better. And lastly, I know she's fuckin' dead," Maybell finished by tossing a piece of corn to Camille first, who caught it midair and then tossed one at the cage. It just cleared the bars at the top and landed in Joey's hair, again. He picked it out and popped it into his mouth.

"Oh yeah, how you *know* that?" Joey asked while he chewed.

"Cuz the last time I went out to get the paypa, she wasn't up my mo'fuckin' ass. Speakin' of ass, that was one of the things she did that just made me dislike her as much as all other people. I jus' don't like people at all, really, because they all do the same shit. But she was the one who lived next door to me, so she got to do silly, irritating shit to me all the time. She was like all the rest when it came to colonoscopies."

"Colonoscopies?" Joey quizzed.

"Oh, hell yeah," Maybell started as she tossed another piece to Camille then to her captive audience. This one caught on the bars, and he plucked it from overhead and stuck it in his mouth. "You are too young to know personally and probably never worked in an office but every time someone would get to be near age fifty, they would start walking around the office to every motha' fucka' they could find and tell 'em, 'yeah, I have an uh-pernt-ment! I have to go get a colonoscopy on Friday', or 'Yeah, it's that time, Imma take some PTO, need to go have my colonoscopy', and 'Well, gotta have my ass checked.' Motha' fucka' I don't give a damn," she tossed another piece at the cage, but it didn't clear the bars this time. She wasn't looking and didn't know, nor care, to toss another one to make up for it. Camille went over and snapped it up while Joey watched.

Maybell kept going, "So, I go outside to get the paypa and here she comes in those same tight-ass white pants and gardenin' gloves,

94

prancin' near the fence, ol' narra' ass. 'Maybell' she says, 'Oh Maybell, hey, um look, you are a little older than me,' but I remind her that I'm not, well I guess I am now. Anyway, she keeps goin', 'um, I gotta have a colonoscopy and I was wondering what advice you might have?', so I tell her I ain't got no advice and from that moment on all I ever see again is her asshole where her mouth should be, all puckered and brown. And that's what happens when people do that. I mean, fuck Joey, people won't tell you how much money they make, where they got a tattoo, or what it looks like, but they can't wait to tell you that some stranger is gone stick a metal rod up day ass."

Maybell sat up and retrieved the cup that was intended for Joey, "Open up, hamsta'." He did so and she was a little more tender this time with the soda pouring in the funnel. Then she tipped the bag of corn to her face and while chewing looked down at her captive as she started to make a face like she was chewing on a slug. "Ew, Joey, dis popcorn be rancid." She poured the rest of the bag on his head and left the room.

16

Duper's Delight

After a short while, Joe heard the television kick on again. This time, Maybell had left the bedroom door open. It sounded like a murder mystery show, though it was turned up loud like a movie. Daylight was starting to fade, the shadow on the floor made him wonder if it was near time for one of those "updates".

He pondered the idea of pushing the cage slightly away from the wall and then contemplated the consequences. However, he knew that his strength was on the downswing. He hadn't slept nor ate well, and he was growing more and more irritated and cramped. His pants were soaked, stinking, and burning his skin from the ammonia in his own urine. *Fuck it*, he thought, *what's she gonna do other than end this or let me go if I cause too much of a ruckus?*

Joey slid slowly and quietly on his side and put his fingers through the bars on the back of the cage. He could touch the wall and still had about two-, to two-and-a-half inches he could push away from it. He decided he would only do an inch or less in between times that Johnson came in. It's like losing weight, when people see you every day, they don't notice the gradual shift. But when people who haven't seen you in a few months show up, they see the weight loss as dramatic; noticeable. Maybell may not notice the small gains of his success if he pulled this off. Then the real task of having to unscrew screws that were all set in metal was still in front of him. He had learned over his years of breaking and entering that those were the most difficult. No matter how far you worked them out, they never were likely to be easy to finger-loosen even near the end of their length. One would have to use a screwdriver to remove them entirely.

This posed another problem, he didn't know how deep they went into the frame. What he did know was that if he could get two screws on one side, or on the bottom, loose enough—and if she left that house—he could kick his way out. But if he got caught, she would likely screw them back in the frame or shoot him dead.

Little by little, quarter inch by quarter inch, Joey pushed against the wall. Each push created a creak, and each creak created a frown, and each frown ended with a pause, and each pause ended with a smile as Joey admired his work.

Maybell started to cackle at whatever she was watching. It encouraged Joey to at least think about trying to get another quarter inch away from the wall, but he thought better of it. Her laugh must have come at the conclusion of a show. What sounded like a reporter came on, although, based on how the sun had just shown its last ray though the window of the bedroom door that led to the backyard, it wasn't yet the 10pm broadcast, she quickly turned down the sound. It was becoming apparent to Joey that she didn't want him hearing the news nor anything that was being reported.

He couldn't figure out why but decided to put no brain power into trying to figure it out.

No one knew he had flown to New Orleans to perform the task he had completed. Maybell may have suspected it, but she obviously hadn't reported it. Although he couldn't see the west side of the house, the side that Gadfly's body was on, he was sure there had been no cops there; not yet anyway. He only knew that he needed to get out before they showed up to find him in that cage, dead or alive. His final thought was that the longer she kept him there, the less likely that she was to turn him in, and the more likely she was to kill him, unless he could kill her first.

Maybell entered the doorway while Joey was lost in the thought that he had tried not to give into regarding the mystery of what was on the news that Maybell was so interested in her hearing and him not.

"You still awake, hamsta' boy?"

"It's not the most comfortable two days I have spent in any house, so yes, I'm still awake."

"Well, I'm sorry. I'm not used to havin' house guests. I guess I jus' dunno how to act. Where's my manners? You kill a he'pless little ol' lady, then try and kill another, not so hep'less one, and expect someone to give you five-star accommodations."

"I thought you didn't like her."

"I thought you didn't kill her."

"I didn't, I don't even know what you are talking about," Joesph finished with a smirk.

"See, that's the thing, felons are the first to complain about how decent folk should act when they, themselves, ya know, the felon, are in the one-down position. Over the years I have seen and read a lot about criminals; always complainin' when cops or detectives or the law is unjust. I don't play that shit. I can't abide it. Once you, as a criminal, as a punk- ass motha' fucka', takes someone's innocent life, they have no rights no mo'. Now, I do believe that people are presumed innocent until proven guilty. But once you are a proven felon, once you are caught in the act, you ain't got shit to say about how law-abiding citizens and the people that protect them are allowed to act toward you—not now, not eva'."

"Isn't it unlawful to hold someone captive?"

"SEE, MY POINT EXACTLY! There you go, proved my pernt right with the first sentence ouch ya mout after I finish! However, to answer yo' dumbass question, you are being held under suspicion of murder! Thing is, I ain't suspicious of shit. I know you done gone and killed Gadfly!"

Joey said nothing as Maybell took a breath and steadied herself to finish, "The second thing is that fuckin' smirk you gave. See, I've read about that, too. I've seen some things about that on my crime doc-u-men-trees. It's called 'dupers delight'. Y'all jus' cain't hep it! Innocent people can be scared as shit when they are under suspicion, guilty people who do things in the heat of the moment can be scared enough to blink when confronted, but it takes a cold-blooded, guilty motha' fucka', to be cocky when confronted about a crime they committed. It's like a proud child, one who wants to tell you how they got into a locked cabinet and pulled the cookies out…ol' rotten-asses!"

Maybell sat on her bed and patted it to let Camille know she could sleep up there again, like the night before.

"So, what are you going to do with me?" Joey finished with no smirk at all.

"Joseph, don't hound me," Maybell scolded while crossing her feet on the bed and picking up her copy of *Helter Skelter*. She went to the page that she kept marked with a plastic sleeve that contained a 1909 T206 Honus Wagner baseball card in mint condition. The one card that Mr. Johnson had held nearly his whole life.

Joey slid down in his cage and drifted off. Later, he woke up to Maybell snoring, her lamp still on, Camille looking over the foot of the bed and right at the stranger in her cage. As much as it seemed to Joey that she wanted to be on that bed and never was allowed to be, for what Joey guessed was years, it appeared she wanted to be in her cage now. Maybell continued to snore, and Camille scootched further off the foot of the bed. Joey quickly shifted his gaze away from her; he didn't want that dog anywhere near him. She hopped down off the bed and was only a few steps away from her cage, his cage—*the* cage. She put her nose to the ground and took a step closer, and Joey just shook his head "no", but she took another step, anyway. Joey realized he couldn't hear a thing as his ears went hot. All he saw was a shadow appear across the floor and as he slowly looked over, he saw Maybell sitting straight up with the gun pointed directly at his head. She spoke in a low, deliberate, and gravelly tone, "Don't chew even look in her direction. She is the only thing in this world keeping you and me alive right now."

Joey put his hand up to acknowledge both his fear of being shot in the face as well as to let her know he had no intention of touching Camille. Maybell patted the bed for Camille to come back up there, "You almost got Hamsta' Boy shot. You stay up here by me, 'ol girl," Maybell put the gun on the bed and turned the light off.

"Night night, Pissy Pants," Maybell mocked. He didn't bother to respond.

17

Where's Gadfly?

All three were awakened by the sound of knocking on the front door. Camille was the first to jump up and over Maybell but stopped in the doorway from the bedroom to the hall and waited for Maybell to get out of bed. Joey was starting to look like four different versions of excrement and waking up with it on his three-days of stubble didn't help.

Maybell stopped and stood at the door as Camille had. Then looking at Joey, put her index finger to her pursed lips in a "shhhhh" pantomime, and smiled slowly in a way that would have given any person the shits. As for Joey, it was no different. She pulled the door at the knob in a slow-motion pace to close it. When it got to her head and touched it, she and the door moved together, her finger still on her lips and that ghoulish smile on her face. After each one of her eyes disappeared, the door finished with a *click*.

Maybell made her way to the front door with Camille behind her. After she reached the front door of the house, she moved the curtain that covered the windowpane and saw two New Orleans police officers. He, the white officer, was looking at the door and then into the window when Maybell's face appeared. The black female was looking back at the street. Maybell's smile was now that of a sweet ol' grandmother as she opened the door to greet them. It opened inward but the glass storm door that opened outwardly was held by the male officer. The name bar on his uniform read 'T. Pinkston'.

"Well, goot mornin'...officer Pinkston," Maybell said after she held up her cheap chained readers but didn't put them on. "What might I do for you this fine mornin'?"

"Good morning, Ms.?"

"Mrs. Johnson. Maybell Johnson."

"Mrs. Johnson... may we come in? We have some questions we would like to ask you. It shouldn't take long."

"Well of course you may," Maybell held the door open wide and waved them in while she let the "how-D-do" smile leave her face when she turned around. She tightened the robe that had her gun in the right pocket and Joey's knife in the left.

"Thank ya', ma'am."

"Well of course! I respect New Orleans finest. And what is your name officer...," she trailed off in question as she turned to look at the female cop.

"Officer Williams, ma'am."

"Officer Williams. Yes, well na', y'all please sit. I ain't put no coffee on yet, y'all want some? I'll make it. Oh, and don't worry none about ol' Camille here, she don't bite nothin' 'cept any type of food you put in front her."

"Aw, no ma'am. We won't take up much of your mornin'. We just wanted to ask you a few questions about your neighbor."

"Oh? Which neighbor?"

Officer Williams opened her note pad and pulled up one of the pens from a pair in her top pocket, then screwed out the ball-point as she answered, "A Mrs. Dorthy Gadfly."

"Oh my, yes. Mrs. Gadfly…has she done something wrong?" Maybell asked clutching pearls that weren't there and looked worried even though she felt nothing of the sort.

Officer Pinkston answered with a slight laugh and shaking his head, "No ma'am, not that we know of. No, um, we were called out on a wellness check and wanted to ask if you knew of her where-a-bouts."

"Well, let me see," Maybell started as she looked up and to the left, "I saw her last…hummm, well, I don't remember the last time I seen her. Maybe a few days ago. She not answering her door? She's a right friendly lady. I'm surprised y'all didn't see her out in the yard doing something with her flowers. Oooo, she jus' love to fuss over her yard. I joke with her all the time about how I wish she would make mine look that nice," Maybell made sure not to slip up and talk about anything to do with Gadfly in the past tense. "Oh, that reminds me, I need to get my cash out. The yard kid comin' tomorra'. I'm sorry, what is a…what ya called it? A 'wellness' check," Maybell asked as if she didn't know what that term meant.

Joey wasn't moving a muscle. *If they come back here Maybell will feign that she is a senile old lady and I'll get life in prison once they find Gadfly. Hair, or fibers or some shit will get me jammed up, no doubt*, he thought.

"Yes ma'am. We knocked and she didn't answer. So, we are asking some of her neighbors when they saw her last. Maybe you know something about her comings and goings."

"Naw, I usually just stay in my house and mind my own bid-ness. The only time I see her is when she in her yard, ya know, fussin' wit' dem flowers."

Officer Williams took over, "So, you wouldn't have a key or know where she might keep a spare one around, would you? Maybe in one of those flower beds?"

"No ma'am, we've ain't neva' been that close. I mean, well, we just chat a little here and there when I get my paypa in the mornin'."

"Mrs. Johnson, we noticed a car on the side of the road, a rental car. Have you noticed it?"

"Oh, yes! I sure have. Like the last two mornin's of gettin' my paypa and mail."

"Do you know who might have left it there?"

"No…ma'am," Maybell had been slowing her speech slightly to be deliberate in her answers.

"Okay, welp, that seems to be it then," Pinkston said with a slap of his leg, "No idea about the car then, right?"

"Right."

"No keys, and no sightings of Mrs. Gadfly that you can remember in the last few days?" Williams finished.

"No ma'am. Look, do y'all think something happened to her?"

"We are about to find out, I think. We are going to have to knock again and then push the door in if she doesn't answer. Her family member that called and said with all that's going on right now, it's odd that she has not called, but they are too far away to check on her themselves."

"Oh my," Maybell clutched her chest again and looked at both officers who paused and held her gaze. "Well, will you please let me know that she alright when you find out?"

"Oh, I'm sure it's just a misunderstanding. We'll check right now and see," Pinkston finished and looked over at his partner who broke her stare at Maybell and looked back at Pinkston. He gave his head a quick nod like, "we're done here".

Officer Williams added, "Well, if you think of anything else please let us know. We'll be right next door."

"Oh, yes ma'am, I sure will," Maybell said as she stood up, walked past the officers, and pushed the storm door open.

Both officers stood up as Pinkston said, "Thanks so much, Mrs. Johnson, we may be in touch."

"I'll be here; that's for sure. You can count on that."

"Oh, you're not leaving town?" Williams asked.

Maybell was a little taken aback by the question and thought they may just be joking, "Naw, I never leave this house but to get the paypa, go make groceries, and go to church."

Williams' interest was piqued. She had seen no crosses, no pictures of Jesus, and no Bible on any surface, "Oh, what church do you attend?"

"Franklin Avenue Baptist."

"Why, yes, that's Pastor Jones, isn't it?"

"I do believe. I hate to admit this, but I haven't been in a few months. I've been a backslidin' Christian."

"I don't judge," Williams said with a smile. "Well, you have a good day, ma'am."

"Y'all too and let me know if I can do anything else to be helpful."

"We sure will," Williams said like she couldn't wait to.

Maybell shut the door and *backslid* a few feet so she could see them through the curtains, but the officers couldn't see her even if they turned back around to look.

Pinkston asked his partner, "Pastor Jones, huh?"

"Yeah, I have no idea what the pastor's name is. I wanted to shake her up. I just know something ain't right with Mrs. Maybell. I'm not saying she has killed anyone. I just get a suspicious feeling about her."

"Well, we'll see what 'ain't right' next door, first."

18

There She Is!

As the cops went down Maybell's stairs, she slid slowly over to the kitchen window on her right. The side of Gadfly's house was in view, though her curtains were drawn, as were Maybell's. However, Maybell could see through the crack in her own blackout drapes that covered the sheer ones that were fully closed. The officers that had just been in her house joined the others that were standing around the rental car and peering inside. Joey had rented it with a fictitious name that matched a credit card and driver's license sent to him by an unknown person who brokered the deal on behalf of some interested parties. After the two cops joined the rest at the car, Pinkston pointed with his thumb over his shoulder toward Maybell's house. All the other cops looked in that direction, but Maybell knew she was far enough in by her other window and couldn't be seen, so she didn't move.

While Joey listened to the faint pounding on the door of a house nearby, and figured, as he allowed his mind to wander, it must be the Gadfly lady's place. He had no idea at the time, nor now, why the people that contacted him wanted a specific person killed, have it look like an accident, and if it went wrong, why he had to pick a random person nearby. He was still regretting that he simply went next door after killing Gadfly. He could have picked another nearby street, instead; not this house, not this woman. At this point he was almost ready to get it over with. He gave it thought when he heard that there were, what he believed, cops asking questions. He was thinking maybe he should just start shouting and kicking to get their attention. Orleans Parish would likely convict him and not Texas. In Louisiana, he could just live out his days in the joint. Only problem was that they were likely to extradite him to Texas where he might get a shot in the arm for some murders he committed in that state because, after they got him on Gadfly, they would have his DNA on file, and they would run it against some cold cases. *At least Texas had let go of the chair in '64*, he thought to himself.

Joey decided to let this play out. When the cops started to pound even louder and shout Gadfly's name, Joey settled on the realization that he wanted to become Joseph again. He wasn't going to just let this lady win. He decided he would take his chances with Maybell and not with the state of Louisiana nor Texas, though, it was a tough call. Even though Joseph was a cold-blooded killer and had done more than one stint in jail and a short one in prison—where had fought a few people—they were men and most of them were large in stature and mean as hell. He was scared each time but refused to show it. Had he shown it, it would have bought him more trouble than he could afford. Although he wasn't as scared now as he had been in those "big boy fights", he was, however, troubled. Joey wasn't scared of the cops even though he could hear them starting to bust through the front door of Gadfly's house. They were about to find her body, throat slit, and a now wilted salad that she had started to eat right before he got there. No, he wasn't scared of the cops. It was Maybell that concerned him most.

As for the people he had killed, and he was not caught for those yet, it was never about anger nor rage nor fear for his life, it was simply business.

He heard Maybell in the front room call back to him, "Wheeeeere's Gadfly?"

Joey heard the door they were trying to get into at Gadfly's house. He had only been able to lock it at the knob, he had no deadbolt key, of course. Then he heard it give way and all the voices in unison when they found her. Joey heard some of the cops as they began to shout a few "Aw fuck's" and one "Oh Jesus!" When the commotion died down, he could hear the retching of one, maybe two, officers when they caught wind of the body.

"There she is!" Maybell mocked, again.

He wasn't concerned nor afraid of any of the consequences he could face because he had killed Gadfly. Joseph knew how to live in the prison system, but he didn't know how to live in a small cage. He didn't know how to live with a woman that he concluded feared nothing. He had also concluded that she was seething with rage underneath all her acting. He almost wanted to know why.

He was too afraid to ask, though.

And for good reason.

He just didn't know how good...

110

Yet.

19

The Cop, The Coroner, And The Investigator

Maybell's house consisted of the front room she and the cops had been, the kitchen, and a short hallway between that kitchen and her bedroom. The hallway was split with a doorway that led to the bathroom. She had backslid further near the hallway and narrated, in real time, the goings-on at the Gadfly residence for Joey. She could see the front stoop of Dorthy's house and the street where he had parked his rental from her position by a tiny kitchen table pushed against the wall. Before she had left the front room window, she had pushed back the blackout curtain a few inches more and left the sheer curtains closed. She could see out, but no one could see in because it was a sunny morning outside and dark inside.

"Joey, they in the house."

"I can tell."

"Hush, boy, or I'll quit telling you what's going on."

"Heard."

"Oh, my little lamb was in the military, no?"

112

Joey didn't answer.

Maybell continued, "Maybe just in a kitchen."

She waited but Joey still didn't answer.

"Here they come. More cops pullin' up. Oh, yeah, looks like a Sergeant. Let's see…yep, there's the stripes. He's a big ol' doofus lookin' fella', pullin' up his britches by the gun belt. Got a few cops coming out the front door. Now they tellin' him and pointin' inside. He's putting something white under his nose. It's that shit that kills the smell of death. Yeah, dat's what it is. Lawd she musta done stunk up the place. I bet her cheap-ass always kept the air conditioner off to save money. I almost feel sorry for her and that's mo' than I can say fo' you. Oh yeah, now they passin' 'round the little jar. All of 'em puttin' that shit on 'cept for that one black lady cop. She's a little hard and she's definitely smart. I don't think she believed me about the church. Yeah, I already like her the most."

Maybell paused for a few seconds before continuing, "They all goin' back in there with Sarge, now. One cop is just stayin' by the door, looks like, I can only see his shoulder. Yeah, he don't want no more of that stank. I think he was one of the ones that shot outta there and started pukin'…rookie-ass."

She was quiet for a few minutes, then continued, "Ya know, there ain't a crime show I ain't seen but it bein' so real, in real time, and right next door, now that's somethin' I never thought I'd see. Well, not again, anyway." Joey had no idea what she meant, and he didn't think he wanted to know.

"Oh yeah, here comes the crime lab van. Little short, white thang. The woman that just got out, not the van, but it's short, too. The van, I mean. Why the crime lab woman always this tiny thang that got her hair in a tight-ass ponytail and a camera that is twice as big is she is? Joey, you think it's part of the job description? Don't answer that," Maybell said with a look over her shoulder toward her little lamb that she couldn't see.

"She goin' in, now. Sarge comin' out with a few others." Maybell paused another minute or two, "Uh oh, there's the crime tape. Yup, we bona fide. We got us a real-life homicide scene now! Shouldn't be much longer before her house is crawlin' with suits an' e'ry thang. Hey, you want somthin' to drank to celebrate the sit-ia-tion?"

"No thanks, I'm good."

"No, you ain't but I take your meanin'."

Maybell got a can of Coke from the fridge, popped the top, and took a long swig as she continued to look out through the window then smacked her lips before she spoke again. "Ya know, I thought about becoming a cop on the days I was tired of my boss's shit at the coffee roasters. But my Ronald worked there, too. And I loved being by him. Yup, worked there until the day he died."

"Is that why you have so much rage?"

"Ain't that a blip? A comment such as that from a killa'."

"I never said I killed anyone."

"You never had to say it."

"If I've ever killed anyone, it was never out of anger."

"Yeah, I didn't think so. This is a bidness fo' you. I wouldn't go so far as to call you a pro-fess-O'nal or nothin', but I don't think you had no personal reason to kill her, and you certainly had no reason to kill me."

"I told you I was coming to rob the place—"

"Let me stop you right there, my little lamb," Maybell continued by speaking over her shoulder, "If that were true, and it ain't, I would know it."

"How would you know?"

"Because you would'a had shit from Gadfly's house either on you, or in yo' car. And you ain't had nothing but a knife, keys, and a paper with her info'mation on it. No, she was targeted, it went bad, and you needed me for a cover but forgot to take shit outta her house to make it look like a robbery."

"Mrs. Johnson."

"Yes, little lamb boy?"

"You should'a been a cop."

"That's detective to you, Joey. OH, and look what I just did! I just spoke them into existence. Here come the suits." Maybell finished the rest of the can with another swig, another smack, and tossed the empty in the trash. She came in the room and looked down at him, "Shit, don't you look pitiful."

She started to walk over to her vanity and Camille's nails clicked on the hardwood floor as she followed her from the hall. Maybell pulled out the chair, sat down, and started to fuss with her hair as she spoke up again, "Well, if you live, at least the next cage you get put in will be bigger than the one you in na'"

"You gonna turn me in?" Joey asked, his Texas drawl more apparent now than ever.

"Pfft, I'll do no such thing," She stopped *poofing* her hair up and looked in his general direction without looking him in the eyes, "Naw, Imma see how this plays out. I mean, I have plans, but they are more general in naytcha'. I don't know what's gone happen to you. I jus' know we gone have some mo' time together."

"What you mean by 'general in nature'"

"I mean nature," Maybell stressed the 'r', "has a way of takin' care of things. My hands will be clean 'nuff. Now, if you get all froggy on me, well, I'll do what I gotta do," she said as she went back to fussing with her hair, "and even then, things can go a few different ways."

"Well, at least you don't sound like you are going to outright kill me."

Maybell pulled her hands away from her head, turned, and this time looked him dead in the eyes, "Oh, I wouldn't count on that."

They both squared off in a gaze.

"Now, quit hounding me, Joey, I have to get ready for my big debut."

After Maybell's thinly veiled threat, Joey had to muster as much courage as he did when he was in that Texas prison to keep from looking scared.

He was startled when Maybell said, "Ol' stank-ass pissy pants."

116

He was glad she said something to lighten the mood even though she wasn't trying to.

Maybell had finished putting on what little makeup she had that was usable and got up from the table, "I jus' knew I should have bought at least some of that makeup from that nice young lady at the mall," she mostly said to herself out loud. Her little lamb had said nothing the rest of the time she had been at the vanity. Camille had been laying at Maybell's side the whole time she was getting ready. She gave the dog a pat and went over to the closet that was between the bedroom door and the cage, then opened it. Joey just kept one eye over toward her because he didn't know what she was going into that closet to retrieve.

She came out with a regular button-down blouse that had flowers on it like the rest and some black pants with creases in the legs. Both were on hangers that one would get at the cleaners. She shut the closet door and left the room with Camille in tow, then went to the bathroom where she changed clothes. Before she did, she picked up the plastic grocery bag that was lining her trash can in the corner between the toilet and the sink and deposited her gun, his knife, and the rental car keys in the bottom. She put the bag that was half full of yuck back in the can and tied it tightly to the rim.

A knock came from the front door and, as if she had been standing in the hall the whole time, she peered around the corner to look at Joey. "Well, look'a' that. Right on time," she said, then finished by telling Camille to "stay" and pulling the bedroom door shut—leaving the mutt and the lamb in the bedroom. Joey heard her shout to the front, "I'M COMIN'!"

Maybell looked through the curtains covering the front door panes of dirty glass. There stood an investigator. He, of course, was wearing a suit but had taken the jacket off. It was a little later in the day now and it was getting hot. There, with his red tie, crisp white shirt, black pants and shined shoes, stood Detective Houston.

He wasn't alone, Office Williams was with him and ready to view a repeat performance of the Magnificent Maybell Johnson. As she opened the door, Houston went right to work, "Ma'am, we are so sorry to bother you. I know the uniformed officers already spoke to you this morning, but I have some terrible news. May we come in?"

"Certainly Detective, um…"

"Houston, ma'am."

"Sure, Detective Houston. I'm Mrs. Johnson, by the way," she said as she opened the storm door to let him in.

"I'm so sorry we had to come back over here but we need to inform you that your neighbor, a Mrs. Gadfly, looks to be the victim of homicide."

Maybell grabbed her ghostly pearls again, "My lawd! You cain't be serious!"

"Oh, yes ma'am, I'm so sorry. Please, please sit," Houston said as he put his hand out toward her shoulder but didn't touch it. Maybell just backed into her tiny coffee table and put her hand on her

118

recliner and then plopped down like she had been gob smacked. Officer Williams almost couldn't help but smirk, but she didn't. She just took in the whole act.

"I jus' feared the worst after the officers lef' and then I heard all the poundin' and hollerin' over there. I was getting ready to go out and run some errands, but I just couldn't shake it. I jus' felt it in my bones. Oh my. I jus' cain't believe it."

"Yes, ma'am. I'm so sorry. Did you know her well?"

Maybell shook her head slowly as if in the deepest of shock, "Naw, I mean she was a nice enough lady and like I told the officers dis mornin', we would speak when I would get the paypa or da mail."

"I know they asked you already this morning, but do you know anything about that rental car out front?"

"Nothing at all, 'cept that it was out there. I ain't sure how long…a few days, I guess. I jus' cain't be sure," Maybell looked up as if she was coming too from being knocked out, "Wait, you think whoever did dis terrible thang is coming back or maybe even still around?"

"Well, ma'am, that's one of the reasons we're here. Did you see anything, hear anything, notice anything out of the ordinary the last few days?"

When Maybell started to answer, Williams just looked around the house slowly. She was scanning for anything that would help her prove her suspicion that ol' Mrs. Johnson knew more than she was letting on. She took noticed of the broken window in the kitchen door. A breeze was causing the curtain to sway lightly.

"Naw, I'm pretty private, ya know. I keeps to myself. I didn't hear nor see nothin' that struck me any kind'a way."

"Yes, ma'am, I totally understand. Do you know if anyone lived with Mrs. Gadfly? Was there a Mr. Gadfly?"

"Naw, he passed many years ago. We, I mean her and I, we both widows. She got some folk that live somewhere in…oh where is that…well, anyway, she got family that live outside the state. I can't even remember the last time they visited, and she never went nowhere but the sto', and to get her hair did, and to the doctor's uh-pernt-ments she was always tellin' me about."

Williams was about to lose her shit. The 'sto'' and 'naw' and 'keeps to myself' that Maybell was putting out there was getting thicker and thicker by the minute. She knew she was smart; she could tell. They both were able to recognize that in one another from the start. Officer Williams kept looking as far back as she could to the hallway and ended her scan at the closed bedroom door. She knew Maybell had been back there and had cleaned herself up in between the time she had come that morning with Pinkston and now with Houston. *But what could she even have back there that would cause her to need to keep the door closed,* Williams thought. *The body is over there. Other neighbors said Maybell lived alone with her dog and didn't talk to anyone. Could she be hiding the person who did this and if so, why? She wouldn't need to shut the door to hide whatever blade caused Gadfly's wounds. Where is her dog, anyway?*

"Mrs. Johnson, may I use your restroom?" Williams asked.

"Oh my, yes, you go right on ahead. It's down the hall to your right."

120

"Where's your dog, ma'am?"

"Oh, you don't need to worry 'bout her none. I lef' Camille in the bedroom this time. Sometimes she like to get all up on people."

"Okay, thank you, ma'am," Williams smiled back and turned to make her way to the bathroom to do nothing more than snoop around. Before she did, she decided to ask about the busted kitchen window, "Oh, and what happened to your kitchen window?"

"Oh gootness, it was so silly. I was passin' a mop in the kitchen, and the handle went right through it."

Williams knew that was a lie. Maybell had cleaned up most of the glass, but Williams noticed how it looked like it had been broken from the outside because there were a few small shards just under the door on the inside.

Officer Williams rounded the corner to the bathroom, slid in, and shut the door quietly. She could hear the detective start to console Maybell and ask more questions. She halfway paid attention to the conversation in the front room and heard Maybell begin to ask the questions, questions about Detective Houston, questions he answered, "Oh, I got into police work because my father was a detective in Huntsville Alabama in the sixties through the eighties before he retired and mom was a lawyer. The law is in my blood."

The modest bathroom had the usual. A sink, a commode, a mirrored medicine cabinet, and a bathtub with a shower head. Of course, the first place she thought to look was behind the shower curtain. Nothing but a grungy green tub that matched the rest of the tile. Then it was on to the cabinet. Pill bottles of innocuous substances, petroleum jelly, muscle rub. Slowly she raised the toilet tank, and there it was. A half empty bottle of whisky laid flat on the bottom. The label was loose and swaying slowly in the water. Williams just rolled her eyes and smiled as she put the top back down as quietly as possible. The porcelain made a scratchy 'clunk' when she slid it back down in place.

Willams put her ear against the wall. She could hear the dog pacing, nails on the wood floor. Click-click. Click-click. Click-click. Then came a sound she couldn't make out. When she tuned into it, the dog began to whine, and the sound instantly stopped. With her head pointed down and left ear against the wall, she saw it: the garbage can.

Officer Williams soft stepped over two feet and leaned down to look into the gray plastic grocery bag liner. Used half-balled up facial tissues appeared to be the bulk of what made up the trash in the can. She pulled out her pen, leaned down closer, and pushed around the tufts of used facial tissue. An empty box that once held a bottle of ibuprofen was in the bottom. Williams had already found the new bottle of pain reliever in the medicine cabinet. She pushed her pen a little deeper and heard a *clunk* and shot straight back up. She instantly knew there was something metal in the bottom of that can that likely shouldn't be there.

Williams flushed the toilet and turned on the sink to buy her self a few more seconds because the bag was tied around the rim of the receptacle and would take time to remove, and it would make a rustling sound if she did. She needed to think because she had no warrant and Maybell was not a suspect. She had no reason to even

122

ask a judge for a warrant and even though it was trash, it wasn't by the curb and thus not city property for all intents and purposes. It would likely be tossed out of court if it even turned out to be anything of probative value at all.

A light knock on the door startled her, "You alright in there? You ain't fall in or nothin', did ya, officer?" Maybell's knock caused the latch of the door that hadn't caught in years to let go of what little grip it had, and the door started to slowly open. Maybell peeked through the crack between the door and jamb.

"There you are. Your detective friend lef'. You good?"

"Gun...belt took a little minute to get back latched."

After holding the police officer's gaze, Maybell said softly, "Oh, those are dreadful heavy things; gun...belts."

Williams felt uneasy, confused, and wasn't sure what she was going to do to get a look in that can. "Yes ma'am, thanks for the use of your facilities," she said as she squeezed back through the door and then past Maybell. Nothing in plain sight looked court worthy and nothing in that bathroom was suspicious other than Maybell being a closet drinker, hiding it from no one other than her dog, and something metal in the bottom of that can. Going to the bathroom was, quite literally, a wash.

"You have a nice day, now, officer," Maybell said to her back with a smile.

"You, too. Stay safe, Mrs. Johnson."

"Thank you, dear heart. You will let me know when you catch that sick sum bitch, won't you?"

Officer Williams stopped in her tracks and turned to face Maybell, "Oh, I promise, you'll be the first to know."

Maybell's smile lowered as she clasped her hands together in front of her.

"God bless you, child."

"Yes, ma'am. May God bless you, too…" Then, turning to the door, Williams finished under her breath, "…with what's coming your way, you gonna need to be blessed."

20

The Elderly New Orleans Debutante

Maybell made her way back to the front door and locked both locks. Returning to her bedroom, Camille nearly knocked her down when she came in. The mutt then went to the back door and scratched.

"Aww naw, honey, not the backyard. We goin' out the front this time, baby girl. Surely is." Maybell turned to Joey and said with the slightest bit of concern, "Now, how you holdin' up little lamb?"

"Seeing as how you are the one answering all the questions and, by the sound of it, even asking some of your own, I'm doing just fine. You're doing all my heavy lifting."

"Keep it up, flattery will get you….well…nowhere with me. But some prison guards like that shit."

Maybell waddled to the side of her bed that Joey couldn't see beneath. She picked up a leash, shook it at him, and smiled. Camille looked over from the back door when Maybell called to her, "Come on here na', Cammy and let momma hook ya up. We goin' out front for my big DAY-bute. Hell, it'll be yours, too, ol' girl."

"Oh, you haven't had enough fun yet, have ya Mrs. Johnson?"

"I'm jus' gettin' started, Mr. Lamb. Ha, I done found me a new playmate," Maybell finished as she hooked Cammy to the leash. Looking over, she thought she detected the slightest bit of sadness in her house guest. Though, it was only her hope as it was not rooted in fact.

"Ahh, now don't you worry none, Punkin', I'll be back before ya know it. Surely will. I jus' want to stick it to that cop one last time before we complete our preparations."

"Preparations for what?"

"What you mean, fo' what? Don't you like surprises?"

"I've been surprised enough by being in this cage."

"There you go again, wit' yo' felonious righteousness. Anyway, me and Camille still have to make our appearance fo' the cameras. You know what's about to happen next, don't cha'?"

"No, and I think I'll just sit whatever it is out."

"See, you do like surprises, after all. Though, should be no surprise what happens next. Com'on baby girl. Let's go get us some press. We gonna go out wit' a bang, ain't we now?"

Maybell's timing was impeccable. Out in the street and spilling onto her and Gadfly's lawn were news reporters from channels

126

four, six, and eight. "Yup, right on schedule," Maybell said as she opened her front door.

The Sergeant was giving his spiel to the press as Maybell exited her house and made her way onto her tiny porch with her love, Camille. She acted as if she didn't even notice all the trucks, reporters, and commotion. The Sergeant was wrapping up as the two ladies sashayed down the front porch steps.

"Ma'am? Excuse me, ma'am," said one of the reporters as she waved over her camera man after she called over to Maybell. "Ma'am, would you be willing to give an on-camera interview?"

"Oh, I dunno, I suppose," she said with an "aw-shucks" smile. This caught the attention of the other reporters, camera crews, and Officer Williams, who looked at the ground and smiled through gritted teeth, "This bitch here," she said with the slightest bit of reverence.

"Roll," the reporter commanded the camera operator who then hoisted the heavy behemoth to his shoulder at seeing her twirl her finger in a rounding motion to signify the movement of tape.

"Ma'am, what is your name and how long have you been Mrs. Gadfly's neighbor?"

"My name is Mrs. Maybell Johnson and I…well, I dunno, we have been neighbors so long I can't hardly remember. I've lived here for decades. I'm widowed now, but my husband, Ronald was his name, Ronald Johnson, of course, we bought this house, oh…let's see…in the early seventies, I think. Anyway, Mrs. Gadfly moved next door in the early eighties, I do believe. Her husband passed away years later. Anyway, we was neighbors fo' decades, I guess."

"And I take it you are aware what occurred here?" By this time, all the cameras were rolling, and all microphones were in her face. Maybell just beamed with delight as she looked over at Officer Williams.

"Unfortunately, I am. But I don't know nothin' 'bout *HOW* what happened, well, happened."

Another reported jumped in the fray, "Did you see anything? Did Mrs. Gadfly have any enemies?"

"Heavens no, at least not that I know of. Now, maybe she had a new boo or someone I didn't know nothin' about involved in comin' and goin'. I never saw no one. But I keeps to myself, ya know—", Her love had become restless with all the excitement, "—settle down, Camille. Lawd, she jus' don't know what to do with herself around all this excitement."

"Ma'am are you, at all, afraid for your life? This person or persons are reported to be still out there, and the police say it's too early in the investigation to have any leads."

"I'm too old to be scared. And Camille here, wellll, she'll just have none of that foolishness, now will ya girl?" she bent down and asked her love while she gave a pat to her head. She hadn't noticed that Camille had just missed being caught on camera doing her business in the middle of the lawn while the gaggle of reporters were asking questions.

"So, you have nothing to add in the way of information that may lead to the capture of the person or persons who committed this alleged murder?"

"Only my thoughts but no proof."

"Would you like to share your thoughts?"

"Only this: There are some good cops and detectives on this case. I have met some of 'em. New Orleans finest," Maybell said as she looked over the large group of reporters' shoulders at Williams who was standing, glaring, arms folded, and face puckered with eyes squinted in suspicion as well as interest in what Mrs. Johnson was going to say next.

"Yes indeed, some fine folks working the case. And I believe they will find the person or persons who did this to my poor neighbor, Mrs. Gadfly," Maybell dropped her smile and part of her act, "But it won't fix nothin'. Cops and detectives show up after a crime has been committed and they, themselves, are only committed until the next crime catches their attention. Ya know, if they don't get a lead in 48-hours, the trail grows cold. And cold cases grow colder and get forgotten. Even if they don't grow cold and they do find the person

involved in this terrible atrocity, they still have a long, long stretch of time before it leads them from captured-by-cop to convicted-by-jury. As you all know, the next big story is only a day or two away."

For Maybell, this was personal, and it wasn't because it was her nosy neighbor's body that was laying cold for the photoshoot going on in the Gadfly house as Maybell spoke. There was going to be more feeling behind her rant as she went on.

"It's always somethin'. Yup, always something that causes good people, who never did nothin' to nobody, to be killed and forgotten. Pfft, and if they do catch the person who did it, and if they killed the person with enough high style and fashion, welllll, the killer gets lauded in the press and immortalized. Gacy, Dahmer, hell, even I'm guilty of being interested in Manson so much that I can tell you more about that time in our criminal history than I can tell you about my neighbor, Mrs. Gadfly. I'm no better. I do what the rest of you do. You see, we all end up havin' to go *through* the murderers to get to the victims. They, the killers, become the gate keepers of their victims' memories. No, no one cares about the victims, themselves. Hell, nobody cared about my…," Maybell trailed off for a moment in memorial and then came back to the present day.

"…THEY become the backdrop to something that we all seem to have in our brains—an interest in the twisted. Car wrecks, we slow down and jam up traffic in the hopes of getting a look at the carnage. Train wrecks? Same thing. Boxing? You're hoping for a knockout, ain't cha'? Car racing? You wanna see a wreck don't cha? Do we really wanna watch three hours of cars doing a left-hand turn when the race is won or lost in the last ten laps? No! They are that long because we hope to see a wreck during one of those turns or every attempt to pass or every blown tire. We have a hunger for blood sport. And we have had that penchant for the morbid long before the Roman Empire and the gladiators. Let me give you another example—"

A reporter started to shout a question, but Maybell was having none of it.

"—ANOTHER! EXAMPLE! Horror movies, there are but a handful of horror movies with a plot worth watching, *Seven* is a personal favorite. I mean, com'on, Brad Pitt and Morgan Freeman? That's a winnin' combination," Maybell said as she started to move her neck like an oscillating fan, "That's good stuff. But most horror movies are garbage. Plot holes you could drive a cement truck through. Like women getting chased and falling in the woods they shouldn't have been near in the first place. Cars that won't start at just the right, or wrong, time. Or how about thinking the smushed faced slasher is dead and dropping your weapon next to his body and turning your back. Ya know, they spend a hunnit grand for every million they make because we just soak it up, live in it! Relish it! Hey, but I ain't no angel," Maybell looked over at her new friend, Williams, who still stood there with arms still folded. She was now flanked by Sarge and Detective Houston. Pinkston was behind her, and his mouth was slightly ajar.

Maybell continued to turn the screw, and so did her little lamb. As long as he could hear her making her plea, for whatever reason he did not know, he would continue to work that belt latch into the Phillips head topped piece of metal on the back of his cage. He knew as soon as he heard her stop, he would either be out the back door or have his belt strapped back though the loops and looking like the good little boy she had come to expect. *Keep on talking, you crazy bitch*, he thought as the buckle slipped out of his hand again, causing him to grab the leather and pull it back through. Each time he dropped it, he would pick it up and go to work again, sweating bullets the whole time.

"Naw, no angel at all. I watch all three of y'all on the television," Maybell motioned to the three reporters from the major local news outlets and continued," I wait to see the body come out the door on a stretcha'. I wait to see the crime tape flappin' in the wind. I try and figure out who the prime suspect is on Dateline before it unfolds. I revel in all the nastiness, too. But I want to believe there is still good in the world. I'm glad we are still a people that likes to see the bad guy get caught," she bellowed. "But it ends there, and we all move on to the next one, don't we? We should all be disgusted with it. But we ain't. It's in our nature. It must be, because it's been around forever and it will continue to be long after this city sinks into the gulf. And it will continue to be long after the Mississippi spews its silt to make another foundation. Another foundation for a new city built on the filth that flows down from the Missouri or maybe some other waterway by then. Ice ages and droughts will come and go; empires will be built and crumble. And millions of years from now, If we last that long, or maybe another society crops up—it'll still be the same. There will be another poor ol' lady, lost without her husband, her family, and nothing but her dog and diminished dreams seen standing on her lawn. Maybe she, too, will be answering questions she has no answers for to a group of people like y'all who are paid to show the world how filthy it is. And maybe they, too, will make and present two-hour murder stories specials but only devote one minute to a human-interest story because, as y'all in the bid'ness say, 'if it bleeds, it leads'."

Maybell came up for air and looked around her lawn that was full of everyone who was there for the murder of Gadfly. Even the little crime photographer had exited the house and was standing there with her eyes wide and mouth hanging open. No one said a single word as Maybell scanned all the blankness in their expressions.

"It's gettin' late, and y'all have to take the time to cut all I said down to fifteen seconds before you run this story. So, with that, I'll say this: I love ya dearly but y'all got to get the fuck off my lawn."

"Ma'am, just one more question before you go," a male reporter said evenly from the back of the pack.

"What!?!"

"As you were speaking, I did a little research on my phone—"

"And?" Maybell quizzed with her eyes bucked up—as usual—when she felt challenged.

"Your maiden name wouldn't happen to be Washington, would it?"

"No! More! Questions! Com'on, Camille. Fuck dez gawkers."

Other reporters turned around to ask the other what Maybell's maiden name had to do with Gadfly or the rant. Maybell didn't even wait to hear what conclusion they were going to come to, because she knew if she did, they would start to ask even more questions. She was saving that part of her story for her little lamb. He had earned it, but she would never let him know that he had. She still had plans for him, as well; the plans were for them both—different, yet the same, in nature. She had decided it would come down to fate. *Whatever happens, happens*, she thought. *Oh, and it's almost time for my update.*

21

On Your Marks

Maybell came in, shut the door, and locked both locks again. She grabbed the remote, turned on the television, and dropped Camille's leash because she was distraught and lost in thought over the mention of her birth name. She knew more knocks would be coming from that door once all those reports were informed of who she was. She wasn't going to answer this time.

Within seconds the knocks she expected did come from those reporters, but she tuned them out. She couldn't even hear the questions as her ears rang hot with anger; anger because she had let her darkness seep out in the full view of, mostly, strangers. *That's what happens when you're a dead lady walkin'*, she thought. She listened to her update with her head near the speaker so she could keep it low, only intermittently looking at the screen. Maybell and Camille's lives hung in the balance, and so did Joey Lamb's.

Joey's fate, to him, felt like it was coming sooner rather than later. He was just getting his belt back on when he heard the mutt scraping her paw against the door like he had any control or permission to let her in. He didn't hear any of Maybell's footfalls coming down the hall, but he rarely did. He was starving, dehydrated, nearly delirious. But he was elated that he had gotten three, solid, forty-five degree turns on one bottom screw while she monologued on the front lawn. He couldn't hear what she said, and he didn't care. He only needed the time, not the information—not the nutty ramblings of an elderly woman, not now, not ever.

After getting his belt secured, Joey got settled into his fetal position and tried to rest. He had smelled the stink so long that he no longer detected it. The sense of smell is an interesting phenomenon, really. One doesn't detect a constant odor over time, it blends in. One then detects the *change* in odors. There had been no changes, so at least he had gotten used to the stench. Either way, it was the least of his worries during the past few days and definitely less than what he would face during the rest of his time with Maybell.

Maybell burst into the room, "You need to eat, pissy pants! I have been neglectful. Even prisoners are not supposed to be starved." Maybell looked down into the funnel hole. It was big enough to get Cheerios through. "Yup, gonna feed ya like a baby. Cereal and milk, funnel face. What 'chew think about that?"

"I'll take just about anything at this point."

"That's the spirit, fawnky britches!"

Maybell went into the kitchen and when Camille turned, the handle of the leash got stuck on the Joey cage. She started to pull to follow Maybell again. Her feet sliding and her nails that were too long were scraping against the floor, but Maybell was still in her fugue state and didn't notice. She turned the radio on just in time to hear the beginning of Led Zeppelin's *When the Levee Breaks*.

"There they are! 'Member how I was telling you about Zeppelin?" She turned it up and kept talking, "Dis your song, Cammy. Hey pissy boy, most white folk can't imagine black folk like Led Zeppelin, but we sure do, 'least the black folk I knew back in the day."

"Oh yeah?" Joey asked back to not let on that Camille was pulling the lamb-cage away from the wall. The sliding was making a horrible racket, though Maybell couldn't hear it. The music from the radio in the kitchen was loud enough, she was far away enough, and she was still lost in her own thoughts. All Joey could think about was her coming back in there and seeing that the cage had been moved and it made him panic in silence. The strap was caught on the bottom of the cage in a way where all the weight and Camille pulling it kept the faux-leather leash taught and he couldn't remove it. That wasn't the real problem. He knew Maybell would understand and was going to call out but ruled against it. However, the problem was, she might inspect the back of that cage and find his handiwork.

"See, it's because it's based on blues. It's blues rock, ya feel me?"

"Um, yeah, MAYBELL, I FEEL YA BUT THE DOG IS PULLING THE CAGE."

"QUIT THAT FUCKIN' YELLIN', LAMB BOY!"

Maybell came around the corner to find the cage almost to the door.

136

"Oh no indeed, not! Get all the way against the back of that cage. I don't want you anywhere near me when I get leash this unhooked."

Joey complied and put his back against the rear of his cell. Doing this allowed him to wrap his hand around the back bar that connected it to the base bracket. He didn't want the weight of his body to make it rattle. She pulled the strap off and went to scoot the cage back but noticed something.

"There it is," Maybell made her way between the cage and the closed closet door, scootching it as she went along like one would opening a letter with their thumb.

Joey could feel the formation of a lump in his throat and his chest tighten. He laughed nervously, "Ya find somethin', what is it?"

Maybell bent down, and her girth made the cage push even further away from the side of the wall. "Yeah, I've been lookin' for this," she finished as she came up with a short-handled screwdriver pinched between her fingers. If Joey could have made a face, he would have. *Mo-ther-FUCK-er*, he thought.

"Hue wee, fuck that be some stank sloshin' 'round in the bottom of that cage. I might as well clean these trays while I got this thang pulled out."

"Naa, that's alright, I've gotten used to it."

"The fuck you talkin' 'bout? Imma change it for me and Camille's sensitive noses."

"Okay, Fine, fine."

"What you gettin' at, Lambchop?"

"I'm just a little hungry and thought we'd eat first."

"Oh, you makin' the rules 'round here now, huh?"

"No no, I just thought—"

"You jus' thought, huh? What you drivin' at? You got somethin' goin' on I need to know about?"

"No, ma'am. Not at all."

"You found a way to pull the bottom out that cage, did'n ya? If I didn't remember I dropped this screwdriver puttin' up new curtain rods this past winter, I'd think you had brought it with you and was up to somethin'."

Relieved that the bottom of the cage was her focus, he was careful not to be too eager to show her, "Ummm, no. I haven't even tried. You got my word."

"Your word ain't worth two balls of goat shit. Scooch around and lemme see, and move them blankets, too."

Joey did as instructed but did it slowly and suspiciously. He believed that if she felt he was hiding something he had been doing to get the bottom loose then she would likely not even look at the back—that was his hope, anyway.

"Move that skinny-ass leg! I want to see the whole bottom. Not yo' ti'ad ass, but the cage. And pull on them bottom slats, too. If there is anything loose in there, Imma shoot you cold dead, you feels me?"

"You ain't gonna find nothin'! I ain't done shit to try and get outta here!"

138

Maybell got cold and low in her delivery, "Don't you neva' take that tone with me, you got it, lamb boy? NEVA'!"

"Yes, Mrs. Johnson."

"That's more like it. Now move yo' otha' leg."

Joey did that, as well. And she looked sideways at him and at the cage.

"Scooch back," Maybell again instructed and started to push the cage with her hips. Joey grabbed the bottom of the back cage wall with his pinky this time. Maybell's view was obscured by the bunched-up blankets. She was able to push it far enough back so that by the next push, and it was her hardest, it smacked the back of the wall, pinching Joey's pinky in place. He didn't make a sound. He had never felt any pain that extreme in his hand before.

If Maybell's bedroom still had the baseboards in place, the legs of the cage would have stopped a half inch from the wall. Joey had noticed they looked to have been removed some time ago. Everything in the past few days that could go wrong, had. Joey had even given thought in that moment that if he got out of this alive, he might consider turning over a new leaf. As Maybell left the room to get the bowls of cereal, he pulled his pinky out slowly so to not make a rattling sound. Just as soon as he did, he got pissed and changed his mind about turning over anything— leaf, branches, nor trunk.

Maybell returned with two bowls, shut the door with her foot, and placed her bowl on the bedside table, careful not to get it too close to her book. The page was still marked by that mint Wagner 1909 baseball card. It was an insurance policy that her husband reminded her every few months during their entire marriage to make sure she hung on to. "Keep it in the protective sleeve, lay it flat, and don't bend the corners," he would tell her. She would always joke back, "Imma bend your corners and lay you flat if you don't quit tellin' me that." It would always earn her a kiss on her forehead.

"Okay, Lambchop, assume the position."

Joey parked his mouth under the funnel spout, and she spooned a little into the opening so that it wouldn't clog. It did anyway, but in the time it took for Maybell to investigate the cage, the Cheerios had become soggy enough for him to suck the mess through. It was the most humiliated he could remember being in many years. There was this one time in prison, but he refused to allow his mind to wander that far.

"Now that's a good little Joey Lamb. Momma Maybell is so proud of you."

And with that, *now* was the most humiliating time in his life.

She gave him a few more bites and said, "Okay, that's enough. I'm over it."

"That makes two of us."

Maybell laid on the bed with her back against the pillows and headboard, then crossed her legs as she took her first bite.

"What you shut the door for?"

"Why, you nervous?" she asked as she investigated her bowl and took another bite.

140

"I've been as nervous as a scolded dog since I saw your pup sitting by the door that night."

"Like I said, ain't her you gotta worry about."

"That's been crystal clear ever since I got that fuckin' skillet 'cross my head."

"What I told you 'bout cursin' in my gotdayum house? Anyway, I shut it cuz they gonna keep knockin' 'til dark and I ain't bout all that noise."

"Why are they going to bother you, of all people?"

"Joseph don't hound me. You jus' mine ya bid'ness."

"How much longer until we get this over with?"

"Get what over with?"

"You keepin' me hostage."

"Hostage? Mothufucka, you break into my house after killin' that nutty bitch next door and you worrin' 'bout how long you gotta be here. Relax yo' ol' stupid-ass. Fate is gone make that decision fo' both of us."

"What is this 'fate' you keep talkin' about?"

"Fate ain't something you can explain, and you educated enough to know that. It'll happen when it happens. And *what* will happen *will* happen *when* it happens. Now, Imma read for a bit so you be quiet."

"You got something I can read, too?"

"Yeah…my mind." The radio was still on in the kitchen and was audible enough that he could tell what was playing. It was James Brown's Sex Machine. "You just listen to the radio and hush. Soul Brotha' Numba' One is on. That's as good as it gets, and it's far betta' than you deserve."

22

Get Set

To Joey, it felt like it was taking forever to fall asleep. Maybell kept the light on and the music going all night, though, when one of those annoying D.J.'s would come on, Joey would strain to try and hear if they were reporting any news, but he couldn't make sense out of any of it, they were talking lower than the music.

Maybell started snoring about an hour after she started reading. At some point she had placed the baseball card back in her book to hold its place, but he didn't know anything about baseball cards and so it didn't strike him one way or the other. He could tell it was an old one and gave thought to stealing it when he got free and killed Maybell. Nothing else in that house, at least of what he had seen thus far, was of any value. Joey settled on the fact that the card probably wasn't worth a shit either, but he thought he might take that old iron skillet for good measure. *Fuck, they probably towed my damned rental*, he thought, *I'll just take her car.*

Joey jolted awake to the sound of a lawn mower firing up. No matter how many times he slept somewhere other than his own house, not even in jail, the lawnmower man always came at 8am. He was never at the place that got the afternoon cut. *Never fucking fails*, he thought. Then it got worse, and for worse reasons.

Maybell smiled from the back door window. She was outside and looking in at him. Maybell tapped the glass with a hammer and shook it around with that spooky grin only she was capable of giving. Then she poked four nails in her mouth and looked at him again. The room started to grow dim as she placed a piece of plywood over the window, and then the nail driving started. The lawn mower was running up and down, going past the window each time. Since the house was raised a few feet and the kid was short, the lawnmower boy couldn't see anything in there. Joey didn't know if he was lucky for that or not. In a few minutes, it wouldn't matter.

After the nail driving on the backdoor stopped, Maybell's face appeared in the window that was up and to the right of the cage and she gave him that same grin. Joey had heard a metal ladder, step stool, or something of the sort a few seconds before he saw her face. He hadn't noticed the night he met Gadfly but was familiar with what was happening next. First, one storm shutter closed. At first glance he could see they were green in color. Then Maybell moved whatever type ladder she was using, the sound was unmistakable now, and then she ascended it again. Her face was now even closer to the cage. She didn't grin this time, she was preoccupied with grabbing the second shutter by the latch. Now the green went to black as she closed and latched it. The hinges creaked and didn't give way easily but eventually it was pitch black

144

except for the sliver of sunlight that came through the small gap where the two shutters met.

Joey quickly stripped off his belt again, pushed the cage away from the wall, and went to work on the same screw as before. This time, the process was quicker. He had had some practice, and he could feel his tomb closing in, his space getting smaller, his time growing shorter. He visualized her setting the house on fire and doing everything she could in advance to make it harder for him to get out. *She must be nailing and latching everything shut. Is she just going to drive off and try and starve me to death? If so, then why did she feed me last night?* he thought.

The lawnmower wasn't as loud now. It wasn't as near and growing fainter as was the sounds of Maybell's deathly construction project; as best Joey could tell, she was going down the entire side of the house, closing all the shutters. At one point he heard nailing again near the kitchen door that he had broken into.

He got the first screw about halfway out. He pushed on the back of the cage to check and see how far it would move if he were to kick it, but it wasn't enough. He decided needed to work on the other side. Joey turned his body and started on the second bottom screw. This time he was slower than the last because he was having to reorient himself for that screw and he didn't have the muscle memory like the last one since he hadn't tried this side yet. And, of course, like all screw jobs, the last one you need to get out is always the one that is hardest to turn, or stuck, or altogether stripped. However, he got it started and smiled with delight; and that's when the Weed Wacker fired up.

Joey hadn't realized how long he had been at his task when the weed-eater cut off, and he heard a kid's voice talking to Maybell. He figured his time had likely run out. He quickly pulled the buckle back through and weaved the leather strap between the loops in his jeans. He was about to get buckled up when he heard Maybell trudging up the back steps and quickly pulled his shirt over it. Maybell entered from the back door; it struck him hard in thought, *Thank Christ! I thought she nailed the damned thing shut.*

"Welp, dat's dat…hey, why you look all spooked, I ain't done nothing to you…yet."

"Not to, well, hound you, but what's with the storm shutters?"

"Lambie, lemme tell ya somethin'. I don't need none of those nosey-ass reporters ruinin' our good time. Don't you think it would be ruined if they was to go peepin' and whatnot?"

"Sounds like they are hounding you worse than I ever could."

"They a close second."

Maybell went to the foot of the hallway, pulled down the stairs to the attic, and shuffled back to the kitchen. Joey Lamb began to hear bags rustling. He heard her start to climb the stairs and watched her legs make it up to the top. She had a jug of water in her hand and used the other to steady herself on the thin railing that was bolted with two brackets to the folding stairs.

"What you putting things up there for?"

"Oh, I jus' like to get my exercise with a heavy jug of water in my hand while I climb the only stairs I own. Up and down, I go," she quipped as she sat the jug on the floor of the attic and slid it as

146

far back as her hammy arm would let her. "Naw, I just put stuff up here because my kitchen is too small and I don't like to go out to the sto' too often, and I always go right when they open up 'cause there is too many people up in there the later I go," Maybell said as she backed down the stairs that moaned under her heft. Camille just laid underneath them and watched her love's activity.

Her little lamb watched, too, as Maybell put more and more items in the attic. Two twelve-packs of soda, more water, an unopened bag of dog food and jars and cans of this and that. Intermittently he could hear her putting items in the fridge, freezer, and cabinets. He figured it was a good sign, too, as she wasn't likely to buy groceries, store them in the attic, and then burn it all down with him inside. He didn't know what the length of those screws were, but he surmised they must be at least a little shorter than the width of the bars that was holding his cell together. He kept up hope that if he could get one more time at that second screw and then thirty or so seconds more, he could kick his way out. But he still had all his work ahead of him if she were home when he decided to take that chance.

Maybell was done with her attic run and put the stairs back up then fed Camille. "Oh, and right on time," she said as she pulled the bedroom tomb shut and went into the living room. The light that shown through the crack of the window shutters was enough to let him know it was time again for her usual "update", whatever that was about. But no matter, he knew she never spent more than five minutes, and sometimes even less, for those updates before she would open the door again. *What's all the fuckin' secrecy about. Those updates couldn't have anything to do with Gadfly. Maybell was "updating" before they even found the body. Something has been going on for days*, Joey thought.

As sure as shit, she opened the door up wide without any notice nor sound of footfalls down that hallway, and Joey was confident that was purposeful. She always acted like she never wanted him to know when she would be coming nor going. Waking up early and slipping out to shop, showing her face in windows so he would never know when she was going to pop up, and poking her head around the door with the shower running—it was all very deliberate.

She went to the closet and pulled out some clothes then announced, "Imma shower. All that yard and attic work got me smellin' myself, both in pride and stank. Oh, you know what, I never did change that cage bottom. But don't go thinkin' I'll be changin' your bottom, like a shitty Pampa'," she said and slid the cage away from the wall with a hard jerk and without notice. Joey grabbed the sides quickly so his body wouldn't shift to the back of the cage and show off the progress he had made before he was ready to do so himself.

Maybell pulled out the first tray and carefully laid it down. She walked to the back door and opened it slowly, looking side to side to see if reporters, cops, or anyone else was out there. Then she went back to the tray and slid it down Joey's freedom path, the path he intended to take once he got the back of that fucking cage kicked out.

While Maybell continued sliding the pan to the edge of the stairs, Joey could see through the open door that there were a few trees lightly swaying and storm clouds rolling in. If she went to the front

148

to watch TV for a while, he might have the cover from the sound of thunder, if he could time it right. Like Andy Dufresne in *The Shawshank Redemption*. Except Andy was innocent—Joey, not so much.

Maybell slid the tray to the stairs, stood to one side, and upturned it halfway—letting all the filth dump out—seemingly without a care in the world about it being right there on the three cement steps.

"Well, that may only help your nose, but Camille is still going to smell it," Joey said as he decided to get a little dig in. He was becoming ornerier by the hour, and more desperate.

"You know, I believe I've given you more credit in the intelligence department than I should have. Your brain don't exactly runneth over with brilliance. I'm startin' to believe that if I lined up ninety-nine fucka's in a row all based on smarts and put you in the line to round it out to a hunnit, yo' ass would be all the way in the back," she finished by pointing up at the sky. "Can't you see we 'bout to get a little rain, Lambie? Fuck sake," she continued as she made her way back up the clean side of the steps and proceeded to pull the second tray.

Maybell completed the task by dumping off that one the same way, then she shut the door. He heard a spray nozzle start and the distant sound of the metal pans being washed out. It took no more than forty-five seconds before he could hear the stream of water on the steps. When she let the trigger go of the nozzle, she shouted through the door, "There, you happy now? Don't answer that," she finished the sentence just as she reopened the door and looked her captive in the eyes. "Now you won't slip on your own urine and

Camille's void as you run out the back door first chance you get, little Lambston."

Maybell pulled the trays up and let them drip a little before hoisting them up the stairs, one in each hand. She shut the door and locked both locks. Bringing the trays over to the cage she noted, "Man, it's like having another pet. This shit is hard work. I think Imma need to get rid of one." As she slid the second tray in, she looked at Camille. "Who you think it ought to be, Camille. Both y'all are lookin' a lil' long in the tooth. Hey, you know where that comes from? Same place as the ol' sayin', 'never look a gift horse in the mouth'. It means that as horses age, their gums recede and make their teeth look longer. It's how you can check a horse's maturity. And if someone gifts you a horse, you just take it. You don't look it in the mouth. But you ain't no fuckin' gif' and I sho' 'nuff ain't gonna' look you in the mowf."

"Yeah, well you ain't no bag of fuckin' cherries, neither."

"You got but one more time to curse in my house before I take care of all my problems with this," Maybell said as she pulled the snub-nosed revolver from her pocket and stuck the short barrel through the bars.

Joey was just about as over all this as she was, "You always say that, but you curse like a street hooker." Joseph was just short of begging for her to do it—end him right there.

"What. Part. Of. *MY HOUSE* are you not getting?"

"Heard."

"Yeah, you from the kitchen. Prison kitchen, not military, wit' yo' 'heard'. If you was military, you most likely would say, 'roger

150

that', and you certainly would have got out dis' fuckin' cage and killed me by now."

"If I was military, you would never have stuck me in this cage to begin with."

"Roger. That."

Maybell put the gun back in her pocket, grabbed her clothes, and left the room. He heard the squeaky handles of the shower and the curtain slide across the metal bar. Unmistakable sound, however, no doors between them were shut and she had pulled that stunt before, looking around the corner when she wanted him to think she was under the water. He was going to leave that belt buckle digging into his hungry stomach for now. He knew the timing wasn't right, just yet, to finish the job.

It was only about ten minutes, he figured, when he heard the water turn off. It was shorter still before she came back in the room, fully dressed. "I got some other things I need to be doin'," Maybell finished by tossing her dirty clothes on the bed and closing the door. He could hear her pull the attic stairs down, again. The creaky springs attached to the ladder quickly gave Maybell's actions away.

Within a few minutes, he could hear her movements in the attic like she had climbed all the way in and was either walking around up there or on her knees sliding things in far corners. If she came down, he would hear those springs as her weight stretched them a little further and the creaking of the thin wooden steps; it was now or never, he figured. He yanked hard and pulled his belt free from his thinning frame. He was resentful that he had to push that fucking cage away from the wall again and he knew he was taking the chance of her noticing this time.

151

He went to work on his life saving project as he felt for the screw and positioned his buckle and the flat ended stem into the slot. Had the screw head been any smaller or the head of the buckle been any wider or not flat at all, he would simply be waiting for death via starvation or by Maybell's hand. Those were two possibilities, but a third was him getting turned in to the local police. He stared at that large brass lock and allowed his eyes to wander to the backdoor. He visualized himself not even touching the steps as he jumped from the opening straight to the fresh cut grass and on to freedom.

He got in another quarter turn, and she was still making noise up top when he dropped the belt. "Fuck," he said through gritted teeth and pursed lips. As before, he pulled the leather taught and slid the buckle back inside, then reset and restarted. But the screw refused to budge any further. It was starting to come out crooked because one of the threads was scarped after his last quarter turn. If he could have screamed and gotten away with it, he would have, and he was starting to consider screaming, regardless. Joey shouldered into the back of the cage just enough to see how much give it had. It wasn't as much on one side as the other, but it was going to have to be enough when the time came. Lambie strapped back up and got in the fetal position again to try and save his strength. He fell asleep quicker than he ever had since being shoved into that stupid cell.

Maybell busied herself in the attic. She put items she didn't want him to see up there. Rope, a loaf of bread, a large flashlight that held a fresh 12-volt battery, a wind-up radio that didn't need batteries, a bag of ice she had bought that morning and stowed in the freezer was now in an old cooler that was already up there. She put some Cokes and a jug of water in with the ice, but there wasn't

152

room for much else. She also included a dog bed that Camille never slept in, so she had put it under the sink two years ago. She removed a can opener and her little lamb's knife from her pocket and laid them on the floor. The gun and the brass lock key she would be keeping in her pocket, for now, anyway. It depended on how things went in the next thirty-six hours, that was as much time as she would give herself. Then, she would make a game time decision regarding Camille, the Lamb, and herself. It was now 10pm on Saturday. She just wanted to get it over with, all of it. Though, she had two more things to do, and they weren't going to get done in the attic.

23

Go!

Joey awoke in a pitch-dark room to howling winds making the shutters snap against their latches and then bang against the windows and the side of the house. He couldn't see anything one foot in front of his face. *Drip, drip, drip.* He was getting wet from water coming from above. He could hear metal scrapping against metal. It was rhythmic, it was almost hypnotic, and it was in time with the dripping water.

A slow clicking sound began coming from the hallway on the left and getting closer. *Click-click, click-click, click-click.* The metallic sound he heard was coming from the right. It was getting louder, too. *Shuck, shuck, shuck.*

The sound from the hallway getting closer still, *click-click, click-CLICK, CLICK---CLICK.* It stopped and he could just make out the shape of the mutt. That clearly meant that Maybell had opened the door. He quickly turned his attention back to the metal-on-metal sound. *Shuck...shuck...shuck.* Three sounds from all three sides and his back was against the wall. Never in his life had he felt so surrounded, so boxed in.

A bolt of lightning struck a transformer on a power pole not fifty yards away from the house and lit up the room through the slit in the rattling storm shutters. There, on the bed, was Maybell with a faraway look in her eyes, they were trained on her little lamb as if she were staring right through his soul, should he have had one. Joey was as rattled as his cage was when he grabbed the bars and pushed all the way to the back. With her axe in one hand and a long-handled knife sharpener from the kitchen knife block in the other, she was sharpening that axe. It was completely rusted; except for the edge of the blade, she had been working for nearly half an hour; her little lamb was ready for the slaughter.

The room went dark just as quickly as it had been lit, and the blade sharpening continued. "You ready to confess?" Maybell asked from the starkness.

Joey knew his time was up. Maybell had some screws loose, but so did he. This was his last chance, and he needed to slow down the plans she had for him.

"Mrs. Johnson, look, you don't need to do this."

"Oh, I think it's time we drop the fo'malities. You may call me Maybell, well, since we in the south, make it Mrs. Maybell," she said as the shucking sound started again.

"Mrs. Maybell, look, I messed up. I should'a never had come here, I should'a never killed Mrs. Gadfly. I should'a done half the things in my life that I have. I'm so sorry. Please, please don't do this, please let me go and you nor anyone else will ever hear from me again."

"What's done is done and someone gotta pay fo' it."

"Okay, I'll turn myself in. I'll confess to everything. I promise!"

"That ain't payment enough."

Another bolt of lightning lit the room. It looked no different than before other than Camille had joined Maybell on the bed and was sitting by her side. Both were staring at the lamb in the cage. He never looked more frightened; felt more scared.

Maybell continued, "No, that ain't gonna work. From my estimation, if you are set free then you are also free to make the same shit choices you always have. Besides, it's too late to set you free, confession or not."

The wind was picking up, and the rattling was getting louder.

"Why?!"

"Because this storm is a bad one."

"What does a bad storm have to do with my freedom?"

"Like I said, it's bad. You can't go out in that, lil' lamb."

"I'll take my chances."

"You already have and, in case you ain't figured it out yet, Camille was named after one of the worst storms eva'. Mr. Johnson and I went through that one. It was a bad one, in 1969, August. After that, me and Mr. Johnson lef' for all the other ones."

"Wait, is this a hurricane and not just some thunderstorm?"

156

"Oh, no, this is just thunderstorms. No hurricane here. Not yet anyway. Now, you ready to talk?"

"I am talkin'."

"No! Not about the weather," Maybell went back to sharpening her axe.

"I said it, didn't I? I said I killed her."

"You didn't say why."

"I was going in to rob the place…"

"STOP THAT FUCKIN' LYIN'," Maybell shouted as another bolt of lightning cracked closer, so close that the light and sound were simultaneous. Her eyes weren't ghostly this time, they were filled with rage.

"Okay, yes, yes…she was a target."

"The fuck she was into enough to be the target of anything other than practice? She weren't no CIA or some shit, was she? If so, I'd have mad respect fo' 'er. That would make more sense 'cause she never seemed all that bright. It was like she was playin' dumb, sometimes. I jus' figured it was her acting like she didn't know she was irritatin' the shit outta me. Was she watching me for some reason? If that's the case, then it would make sense why you needed to off me too, but I ain't nobody. She wasn't watching me fo' nothin'. I may have a past but it ain't nothing like something that the gub'ment would be watching me fo'."

Joey was trying to keep her talking, "A past like what?"

"Oh please…"

"No, really. I wanna know. Look, Mrs. Maybell, you are not like any other woman I have ever met. You are angry one minute and then making fun the next. You read about Manson; you stood outside with cops and reporters and gave some sort of speech while you had me in the house in this fu….in this cage and all that takes guts. Or it takes a person that doesn't care what happens to them but wants to risk it and say something that is important to them. So, please, go on an' say it."

Maybell quit sharpening the axe and started to make a gurgling noise.

"Mrs. Maybell? MAYBELL, WHAT'S WRONG?"

"Oh no, I think…I think it's my heart. Oh, shit this is some kind'a fucked up timin'. Aw fuck, my chest, it…it feel like thay's an elephant standing on it. I..I can't breav' Ahhh fuck shit be hurtin'!"

Lamb boy heard more gurgling.

Joey waited to see if this was his eleventh-hour execution stay, his reprieve, his path to freedom.

"Maybell? Maybell!"

Maybell slumped back onto the bed, and the axe hit the floor with a chunky thud.

"MAYBELL?"

No answer. Just some whimpers and whines from Camille.

"Ohhhh fuuuuck," Joseph said as he began to bump the cage up and down to get close to the axe and away from that wall. He quickly began to contort himself so that he might turn around and begin to kick his way out. Once in position, he grabbed as tight as he could to the top of the cage and, with all his might, kicked at the back of that fucker. BANG! BANG! BANG! The screws pushed out a little further.

Then he heard it, a cackle. Slow and soft at first, then louder. He could here that laughing getting louder because she was slowly sitting up.

"MAYBELL! YOU OKAY?"

"It's Mrs. Johnson now because the fo'malities are back in full force. I tol' you 'bout cursing in my house. Pfft. Heart attack. Bitch please. You can't kill bad grass. That's why I ain't killed you yet. You bad grass. And, well, other reasons. Thinkin' 'bout leaving that up to fate and naytcha. Naytcha has a way of settlin' the score, makin' things right. Anyway, you think you was gone keep me talkin' and gain my sympathy? No indeed not."

And just like that, he was Joey, again. He was beat down, and he didn't care anymore. Any manhood he had left before he walked into that house was now gone. He wanted her to do her worst. The wind howled, the shutters slapped, and he spun around to find her standing over his wire box, axe in hand.

"YOU'RE FUCKIN' CRAZY! I DON'T GIVE A FROG'S FLYIN' FAT ASS WHAT YOU DO WITH THOSE PORK PIE FINGERS OF YOURS! SHOOT ME, CUT ME UP, AND HIDE ME IN THE ATTIC. DO IT, BITCH! GO ON AN' DO IT!"

"Wheeeeere's Joseph? Wheeeeere is he? THERE HE IS! PEEK-A-BOO!"

Maybell swung the axe on the top of the cage so hard it made sparks as Joey played duck and cover with his hands above his head as if it would have made a difference were there no wire there to protect him from that axe. There was still a gun and a crazy ol' lady in play.

In an act of dominance, Maybell pushed the cage back where it had always been and the lamb felt the water dripping on his head again, only now it was in quicker succession. She plopped the axe on top of the cage.

"Now, keep yo' sammich clamps off'a dem bars!"

Maybell turned and left the room.

24

Catharsis

Camille eased off the bed and clicked away behind her love. The water was now dripping on the blade of the axe spattering the liquid over the entire cage. Joey was beat again. But at least she still hadn't noticed the damage to the back of the cage from his kicking because it was still pitch black in the room, but lightning lit it every minute or so. Joey wondered if the storm was passing as the thunder started to trail the lighting, each time growing further apart from the flashes. The cage, of course, was mashed against the wall again, holding it in place, and the axe was in reach. He lifted up his finger just to touch it to make sure any of this hell was real. Joey found both to be real, the axe and the hell.

Maybell returned with something in each hand and sat one item that looked to be a glass jar on the bed. She pulled a small penlight from her pocket, turned it on, and poked the end of it in her mouth. She then walked over and opened the closet door. From what Joey could tell, it looked to be a large container in her other hand, but he wasn't sure. Maybell threw it on the bed once she was in the closet and realized she didn't need it where she was standing.

Maybell pulled down her box of pictures and walked them over to the bed. She opened the box and took out her mall picture, a handwritten obituary that she had planned to have typed up but had run out of time. Then she picked through the rest of her pictures so she could find all the ones of her love, Ronald, and a few more of the rest of her family. She placed them in the plastic container as she went along. She went back to the closet and pulled out the red pantsuit, the belt, and the hatbox. After placing them on the bed, she went back for the black shoes she already owned before the day of her mall trip and placed them on the bed, as well. Joey just watched her like a slow-motion tennis match going to and from the closet, but he didn't dare ask a question.

She kept the large plastic container open and finished putting the items she had collected inside. She decided the hat wouldn't leave her enough room and it would get wrinkled anyway, so she left it out. Next, she placed the copy of *Helter Skelter* with the baseball card that, at her last check, was worth a quarter million dollars or more. She had kept her promise and left it sealed in the sleeve and bent no corners, "That's my little Ms. May" she could hear Ronald whisper in her ear. She closed the Tupperware and traced the top edge all the way around the rectangular box while pressing in to make sure she had a tight seal. Taking the largest Ziplock bag they make from her pocket; she put the Tupperware in it and sealed it equally as well. Sitting back on the bed she turned off her penlight.

With a snap, a flame lit the room, and Maybell touched the wooden match to the first of three wicks of the cinnamon scented jar candle she held in her other hand. After all three of the wicks were lit, Maybell sat the candle on the floor and looked up to the haggard, scared, and malnourished sacrificial lamb. She then sat back on the bed and Camille joined her. Maybell pulled a whiskey bottle from her other pocket, the same one she had hidden in the toilet tank, unscrewed the cap, and tipped it back—taking two gulps. After sitting it on the nightstand, she clasped her hands and placed them in her lap, kept her eyes trained on the candle, and then began to speak, calmly and softly.

"No, Joseph, I'm not crazy. I'm actually quite lucid. You see, here's the deal, this time with you has been cathartic for me. I have avoided people for years because they talk too much but say nothing, to loosely quote the Godfather of Soul. But you've been stuck here; forced to be silent and forced to listen. More to the point, I have been stuck here with you. Stuck with you just as I have been stuck with my darkness much of my life. You are, quite simply, a representation of that darkness."

Maybell looked directly at Joseph, "I've not been raving like a lunatic. I've been venting. I've been releasing all this pent-up frustration about the world, what it did to my family, and getting to do it with one of the main people who have made it that way, a criminal. And, without a doubt, you are most definitely a criminal; cold and calculating. You're clearly in the business of killing people, whom you don't even know, for money. That is my guess in our little game of Clue. I don't know that I will ever fully understand your reason for killing Dorthy Gadfly. But I know she was more of a threat to me than she ever was to you. She could easily have talked me to death," Maybell finished with another swig of whisky. "I may know someday what happened, I suppose."

Looking directly into his eyes, Maybell asked, "Do you know what code switching is, Mr. Joseph Lee Caruso?"

He shook his head and responded, "No ma'am."

"Code switching is when people talk in a way that fits who they are speaking to. Like language, or in our case, a dialect leading you to believe I am who I want you to believe I am. I wanted you to believe you were speaking to an undedicated southern woman. Well, more than uneducated, just plain stupid. The 'crazy', as you called me, part had more to do with the rage I feel. You got that part correct. But more to the point, code switching is about speech patterns. If I had friends—and, to be fair, at one point I did—we would all talk to one another in the same way. Cutting off the 'r's and 'g's in words made us all feel more comfortable; made our jokes funnier.

When I was younger and Jim Crow laws were still in full effect, we could speak educated around educated people; we didn't need school for that. We just copied what we heard the other's say. If we were around educated *white* folk, we just wouldn't speak at all. Now, speaking proper around some folk of any color, even today, can get you marked as thinking you are better than. 'Talkin' like white folk' is what some called it back then. 'All 'uppity' or boujee as they say these days."

Maybell drew a deep breath as she redried herself emotionally for the story she was about to tell, "So, as a black person, myself and others before and after us, quickly learned that you just didn't do that. Therefore, you would just switch your speech patterns back and forth. However, my natural way of speaking is not how I'm speaking to you now. If I speak to Cammy, I speak to her how I feel most comfortable and what takes the least amount of effort on my part. If I'm at the mall or at the grocery store and I am trying to get something I want either cheaper or for free, I speak like an elderly woman who is just kind of confused. If I want to call someone out for treating me… well, you get my pernt. That's not as important to me as some of the other things I'm going to share with you until this storm passes. Then, we'll see where we go from there."

From her cardboard banker's box, Maybell retrieved a picture that she had intentionally left out of the Tupperware and then held it up. It was a black and white photo, though hard to tell from the low light and distance, Joesph thought looked like a stunningly beautiful black girl or woman. Maybell took another deep breath and began to tell her story; the story she had wanted to get out of her and into her sacrificial lamb.

"In 1946, my sister, Jamielynn Washington…well, momma and I, we called her Jamie, worked at the home of a very wealthy and influential New Orleans family. She was only allowed to work in the kitchen and not the front of the house, so to speak. She had not yet made her sixteenth birthday when all I'm about to tell you started. She quit school when we continued to fall on hard times. Each time we fell, we fell hardener. I was young, just seven and my father struggled to find work after the depression. Back then they said, 'If white people get a cold, black people get the flu'. It was harder for black folk to recover from the depression, and we weren't shit before that, financially speaking. My father fell off the sobriety wagon and went to drinking again, then he just fell off all together. I could just never understand how someone could be so broke in pocket but still find ways to have enough money to drink because of their break in spirit," Maybell finished as she shook her head and sighed.

"That left my momma to raise two daughters on her own. She struggled to find a second job, but she did. It was a housemaid's job, like most of the black women in New Orleans in those days. Oh, there were other jobs for black women then. But they were very hard to get, and momma didn't have any formal education, though she was wise, and it didn't pay much but it had its benefits because it was for the same family as my sister worked for. Anyway, I kept at school because that was the deal. I had just started the second grade."

Maybell picked up the bottle and took another swig. She held it up toward Joseph and shook it back and forth. He nodded and put his mouth under the spout of the funnel. The rainwater was still spattering the cage as each drop continued to hit the axe head. Maybell got off the bed, and she poured the equivalent of a jigger in the funnel. Joe caught every drop and nodded his head in appreciation. She sat the bottle back on the nightstand and herself back on the edge of the bed before continuing.

"At that time in New Orleans, Jim Crow was still in effect, like I mentioned, as it was many other places. I didn't ask you before but are you familiar with Jim Crow laws, Mr. Caruso?"

Again, he shook his head no but spoke, "I mean, I only know that it put some things in place that made it harder for blacks to vote."

"True, however, it was more than that. It was 'separate but equal'…so basically, segregation. It was a way to keep black folk in their place. One of the understated but overarching truths was that it manufactured a feeling amongst whites that they were allowed to do whatever they cared to with blacks, especially white men and their treatment of black women."

Maybell needed a moment to collect herself because she was about to break a dam and create a flood that she had never allowed to wash over her in 30 years.

"The people who Jamielynn and my momma worked for were the Donners. There was Mrs. Emily and her two sons, both in their mid to late teens, Bradley and Dudley—stupid names, really. Anyway, they were twins, and then there was their father, Robert Donner. He had taken over the shipping business from his father when he came back from World War II. He and Emily had been married before the attack on Pearl Harbor and had the boys and, well, you get the math."

Maybell began to fidget with her hands. Joseph was letting the swig on his empty stomach take hold and enjoyed being in a little less pain, so he didn't move an inch in fear of losing his comfort—like when one's headache is nearly gone and they move, and it becomes a dull irritation for the rest of the day. Camille had fallen asleep.

Maybell looked at the picture lovingly with a smile and then laid it back down. She faced Joseph again, "Jamielynn was stunning. But, I looked up to her because she was older; smarter. She worked for the Donner's in their kitchen with their other hired lady, a woman from Ireland named Maggie. The two got along well and Maggie taught Jamie something new every day about that kitchen and cooking in general. Sis and momma got hired on because Mr. Donner, ever since being home from the war, held business parties to increase his stature and revenue, and was demanding of a perfectly kept home—at least that is what I came to understand." Maybell touched her foot to the jar candle on the floor just enough to unintentionally shift the light.

The noise outside was deafening. Lightning, thunder, whipping wind, the dripping from the ceiling, and the story Maybell was telling increased Joey's angst and anger. He wanted out of that cage now more than ever. He pictured her getting close enough to him so that he might grab her pocket and pinch the gun out. The more Maybell spoke the more he imagined what she would look like filled with holes and bleeding in the candlelight until they found her. He thought about how she would stink and swell. He thought about how Camille would most likely begin to eat her when the mutt started to starve. Maybell broke his morbid concentration on the possibilities of what he could do rather than the story that was about to unfold.

"He took a liking to her quickly—momma, that is. At least that is what I learned by listening to the two speak in hushed tones and code when momma got home and I had my face in schoolbooks. Sissy—I called Jamielynn Sissy sometimes—Sissy would get home first and start dinner with what she learned that day and some of the scraps that Miss Maggie would wrap in wax paper and have Jamielynn hide under her dress." Maybell looked down and to her right with her head slightly cocked as she smiled, "She would let me help before momma got home. She knew that momma wanted me to keep my focus on school and not domestication. She told me on more than one occasion, 'In the future, something to do with counting numbers and figurin' 'em all out, that's where the money gone be at. I don't know how I know, but I know it will. I don't never want you to have to go dependin' on a man. They ain't worth shit when times is tough and they sure ain't worth shit when another woman come 'long and start tapdancing all up in their nose'!" She let out a one grunt guffaw then quickly went solemn, "But not my Ronald. I have never met a man so perfect. Not before

168

I met him, not during our life together, nor since his passing, have I ever met a man that was more devoted to a woman, and I was lucky that, for a little over 30 years, I was that woman," Maybell pulled herself back together after starting to get tearful.

"We met at the coffee plant. I was a bookkeeper. So, I guess momma was right, it was those numbers that helped pay the bills. But for a time, I just kept living with her. Ronald was on the line, watching the coffee cans go round and round. Getting filled with the ground up beans. You think you would get tired of smelling coffee and stop drinking it, but you don't. Ronald and I never did, anyway. They opened that plant in 1960 and I was twenty-one and he was twenty-four. He saw me walk to the foreman's office one day and I didn't even know he was looking at me. Before I knew it, he was finding reasons to come around, silly reasons, really. They didn't make any sense, but that didn't matter to me. When I thought it had been too long in a day and I hadn't seen him, I would seek him out and ask him silly questions, too. Questions like, 'Does this look like an eight with the circle not finished or is it a five with too much circle?' then I would look up at him all doe-y eyed and innocent. He would just look at the paper and then at me," Maybell paused tearfully as she visualized the memory of her Ronald.

"We did that dance several times before he asked me out. We got married within six months, lived for a time in an apartment, and then bought this house. He got promoted twice and he said I could quit working if I wanted to. We weren't going to have kids, and I wasn't making but about shit-fifty an hour, anyway. So, I quit that bookkeeping job and got cable, instead. I made sure Mr. Johnson always had what he needed when he came home. *Keep a man fat, dumb, and happy and he won't go nowhere* is what he told me. I knew how much he loved me and knew he wasn't going nowhere, no how. I'd gotten into watching all the shows I could about people like you. People who kill people without a care in the world."

Joseph thought to himself, *Yeah, you'll be one of 'em you crazy bitch. I'm going to get out of this cage and smash your skull in.*

Maybell let the silence of her voice fill the air for several seconds while the noise of things hitting the house boomed before she spoke again. "I know you want to kill me, Joseph. I have done what no man can stand for a woman to do. I've emasculated you by making you helpless. I've made you scared. I've made you question how much of a man you really are," Maybell pulled out the revolver from her pocket and sat it on her left because Camille was on her right. Maybell was right-handed but figured no matter how fast he moved, he couldn't get to her as quick as she could get to that .38 even if the door to his cage was wide open. He didn't say a word, not this time.

She continued her story by looking up at the ceiling and blinking out tears as she spoke next, "But it was nature that took him from me, not anyone like you. It was just a bad heart problem inside of a man with a perfect emotional one," Then Maybell flipped a switch and became hard again.

"My sister used to call me her Iron Fleur-de-lis. Do you know what a Fleur-de-lis is, Joseph?"

He gnashed his teeth in response, "Yes. It's on the helmet of the New Orleans Saints."

"You know, most people who live in New Orleans can't even imagine what it would be like to not know, nor do they ever

170

remember a time when they didn't. They are a symbol that represents many things. Primarily, a lily flower but also religious and monarchy symbolism. Anyway, my sister, Jamielynn used call me that. Said I was tough as iron but as pretty as a flower. As one of those two descriptions got more pronounced, the other became less true. I'll let you guess which one on your own as it's only *part* of my point," Maybell said with that creepy grin.

"Back to my sister and our time together. She would teach me what Ms. Maggie had taught her about cooking throughout that day. While she did, we talked a lot about what it would be like for her and I to own our own New Orleans restaurant. We talked about the types of food we would cook just as much as we talked about the kinds we wouldn't. What the place would look like. How we were going to get enough money together to even open a place. At that time though, we would have play menus. Sometimes, when momma would get home, I would pretend to be the waitress and take her order for the only thing that sissy had cooked. I'd speak all proper and momma would giggle. On special occasions, we would even do it by candlelight," Maybell motioned with her head toward the candle on the floor. "I got good at cooking—really good. But ever since Mr. Johnson died, I really don't cook much anymore," Maybell finished with a shrug of her shoulders and a look down the hall toward the noise of something tearing off the front of the house.

The storm was still raging.

Joseph spoke up, "This is one hell of a thunderstorm, and the wind is clearly not the kind I would expect to be—"

"It doesn't matter, and I'm not done with my story yet. See, Robert Donner, like I said, took a liking to my mom. Mr. Caruso, you probably can't imagine what it must have been like for her. Then my Sissy was dead."

Joseph was more interested in her story now. But it was only because it had to with the death of a young girl and that young girl happened to be Maybell's sister. And that made him happy.

"Wait, what do you mean? I thought you said it was your mother he was into."

"That is what I said, Mr. Caruso, and that is what it was. But it wasn't my mother that ended up dead because that's not how the story unfolded. Donner, because fuck his first name, started doing what their kind often did to the house help. It starts when there is no Mrs. around, they find reasons to have themselves served in bed while sporting an erection. Making comments about *brown sugar* and whatnot, you know, just to see how far they can get without much force nor mess. I heard much of this from my momma as the trial that went on."

Maybell waited a second, gathered herself, and looked up, "Before I go on, I want to make sure you understand one thing, Mr. Caruso. This isn't about a black or white thing for me. You are a white man out of Texas and I'm a woman of color from New Orleans. So, I want you to know that you are not in that cage because of slavery or racial ideations. Slavery was around long before the cotton trade or, for that matter, America. And we, 'we' meaning black people, are not even the latest recipients of it, and 'it' being slavery. Girls are trafficked as we speak, girls of any color. If anything, it's more about women and men in general and the lies told to keep that power structure in place, just like Jim Crow. Some may even argue the bible has done that for nearly two thousand years, but that's a longer story and an even longer debate, and we don't have that kind of time. No, you are not in that cage for any of those injustices. For me, it's about criminal justice and it's about you being the unlucky recipient of my unresolved rage, loss, and let's be honest, you threatened my life. One that when I met you, I wasn't sure what I was going to do with the rest of. No, you are a mere representation of part of what's wrong in my world—THE world—and the next question I'm going to pose to you is not because I've deluded myself enough to believe that a psychopath will have any sympathy for me nor the rest of this story."

"So, what's your question?"

"My question is: should I go on?"

"Do you mean 'go on telling your story' or 'go on living'."

"Aren't both one in the same?"

"I suppose they are, Mrs. Johnson, so please continue doing both."

Was her question really about suicide? he asked himself. He concluded that if she were to kill herself, she would most certainly kill him first. Anything that kept them both alive a little longer was going to work for him.

Maybell still had her captive audience and had never told her story to anyone, not even to Mr. Johnson. Her unresolved rage, her darkness, her fascination with death at the hands of others, and what made them tick, long ago made her convinced that she would never allow herself to die by any means other than nature or by her own hand. In this moment, both possibilities were in play. Though, just as she had told Joseph, Cammy was the only thing keeping them both alive, and nature had been on that mutt's side for years.

But the storm was nearing its peak within her, and without her. The wind was howling, and rain bands were beating on the old house. It rattled everything loose and loosened everything not yet rattling. Maybell had held his gaze after he answered her question, and it was making Joseph feel uneasy.

Joey spoke up, "How long did you say this house has been here?"

"I didn't."

"These houses are built on a few feet of cinderblock underneath, aren't they? It doesn't feel stable."

"Hurricanes tend to make things feel unstable no matter how well they are built."

"So, this *is* a hurricane. Why didn't you tell me?"

"Fate and nature."

"You are going to let me sit in this fuckin' cage and—"

"I told you about cursing in my house."

"And I told you you're fuckin' crazy!"

"And I haven't finished my story yet to explain that I ain't crazy, bitchass."

"Let's get this shit over with!"

"I'm trying to, but you interrupted me."

174

"I mean shoot me, you stupid cunt!"

"Not even if your life depended on it."

"Well, yours might."

Maybell, sighed and rolled her eyes, "Anyway, so momma and Sissy were working at the mansion—"

Joseph grabbed each side of the bars, pushed his face into them, and gritted his teeth, "I'm not going to listen to any more of this stupid-ass shit! I already know how this story is going to end! Rich dude is going to rape your mother, and your sister is going to try and save her and the—"

Maybell picked up the candle and tossed the hot wax in his face. Joey wailed, pushed himself toward the rear of the cage, and the loose back shifted. Maybell saw it as Camille left the room without so much as a yip.

"Oooo, my lil' lamb has been busy. My my, I knew I should have took that belt off you," She said because she instantly knew how he had been using it. "Give it up. Give me that fuckin' belt and if you lucky I won't hang you with it!"

"Fuck you! You rancid piece of fatback!"

Maybell spoke softly, "Oh my, there you go cursin' again. Imma let that one slide because I liked that insult. Imma steal that one. It's the only thing Imma steal from you, except fo' that belt. If you live through the night, I'll even let you have it back."

Joey was wiping his eyes and shaking his head.

"Uh oh, you can't see no more, can ya? HOW MUCH IS THAT DOGGY IN THE WINDOW?"

Joey grabbed the cage at the top and lifted himself up and down in a fit of rage, "LET ME OUT OF THIS MOTHER FUCKING CAGE!"

Maybell, picked up the candle, sat herself back on the edge of the bed and picked the dried wax from the three wicks, "Simma down now, little lamb. Take off that belt and give it over or you'll get a bullet in the knee cap."

Joey couldn't open his eyes and, again, felt the truth that he was clearly defeated. He slowly took his belt off and snaked it through the cage.

Maybell didn't collect it but, instead, continued, "Now, where was I...oh yes, so the stuff momma told me about the trial...however, that's getting ahead of myself." She relit the candle and sat it on the floor again.

Joey just held his head in his hands. He was totally beat down, and both knew it.

"Anyway, it didn't happen the way you assumed. The ol' bastard was doing whatever he could to get to momma. He started grabbing her hand and pulling her near and whatnot. He would smack her on the ass when no one was looking. Except his sons, I came to understand that he didn't mind that. He didn't mind his sons being around and seeing how he treated my momma. It was the sins of the father that killed my sister."

Maybell started to tear up again and sighed, "Everyone was home. Mr. and Mrs. Disgusting and the garbage twins, Bradly and

176

Dudley were all there. It was a Saturday and Sissy was in the kitchen with Maggie. The two old fuckers were in the back yard having coffee or some shit. Momma went up to make the beds. She went to Bradly's room first and, by all accounts, he started chatting her up as she was making his bed, picking up his dirty clothes and putting them in the hamper or whatever. I only know what little bits she told me over the years. She tried to just, ya know, keep it movin'. So, she goes to his brother's room, dingleberry douche canoe number two and Bradly followed her and keeps talking about stupid stuff. At some point both boys end up in the room together. Canoe number two shuts the door and momma hears the click of the lock. But she ignored it and kept doing whatever she was doing, I think she said she was making the bed and was bent over. Then she feels a slap on her behind. She said she wasn't going to finish but when she tried to leave, Bradly stood in front of the door and Dudley said something like, 'finish the bed and then you can leave'. She gave it some thought and turned around to tightened up the corners of the bedding or whatever. Dudley pushed her down, flat faced, on the bed. She doesn't know which one was which, but one held her by the wrists and one got behind her and did his best. But there was a problem. He couldn't, well, ya know, get things going and momma started laughing. When I was older, she told me she said, 'Whatsa madda, lil' man, you can't get it up'. Heh! He kept on trying, though. And she kept laughing and it must have made it worse. The one that was holding her writs punched her in the face and that was it. She started kickin' and screamin' and cussin' up a storm. So…" Maybell sighed and looked up and started to choke back tears, "…so they started to beat on her harder and tussle with her. Well, my sister, who was still in the kitchen heard what was going on. Maggie, during the trial, said that Sissy called

177

for momma and started to go up there, but Maggie grabbed her arm and shook her head 'no'. Jamie broke loose and ran up there. It was several against one. Two of them were in the room and history and all the rest of them were in them boys' heads. They say that sissy must have used a hair pin and picked the lock, but it took forever. Once she got in there she got to one of the boys and took him down in her rage. The other boy, we'll never know which was which, jumped on her."

Maybell had never shown so much emotion to a stranger, blind or otherwise. Tears streaming down her candle lit face as she looked up to the heavens and listened as the wind whipped around the outside of the house and the rain smashed into every surface, "She…uh…Jamie was fightin' 'em off both her and momma. They were everywhere…yeah. Momma heard that asshole of a father shout 'STOP' and then out stepped Mrs. Donner and…and she just shot. She just fuckin' shot my sister. Momma saw it all." Maybell finished and took a moment to collect herself.

"Well, anyway, it had to go to trial. Neighbors heard all the commotion and a couple of them testified—Maggie did, too. They were all called liars, especially my momma. They called her a Jezebel and said that she lured those boys into debauchery. The boys said she always had her way with them—both of 'em said that. Cocksuckers. Then they had the nerve to lie on my sister and said she was jealous and that's why she had burst into the room. Then came the real crock O' shit, that Mr. Donner said that he was actually the one that shot my momma to protect his boys because Jamielynn had brought a knife from the kitchen. But that wasn't true, and Maggie testified that it wasn't. They had placed that knife

in her lifeless hand before the authorities got there. FUCK!"
Maybell waited until she could speak again.

"After Mrs. Donner was found not guilty, and all the rest weren't
even charged, the Donners went on with their lives as if none of it
ever happened. They fired Ms. Maggie, of course. Not that it would
have mattered, because she never would have worked there again,
anyway. She kept in touch with Momma for a short time, but their
connection faded away, just like my momma did. She tried to work
other places. Each time it was hard to even get the job because
everyone in the community knew her…but the few jobs she did get,
if she got a funny feeling or something was said that made her
uncomfortable, she would just quit. I kept at school, settled in, and
got good grades, but it was all too much for Momma. I found her
when I was in my late teens. She had taken as many sleeping pills
as humanly possible that day, then took a few more. She left herself
for me to find, though, not intentionally. So, the Donner boys got to
her after all, but they weren't going to get me…and neither are
you."

Maybell just stopped and stared at the candle.

Joey broke the two-minute old verbal silence and said, "So,
what's all this got to do with me?"

"It's like a free pass, regardless of what I decide to do with you.
You see, Joey, all cages are man-made, to some extent. Some of
them we make for others, some are made for us *by* others, and some
we make for ourselves with the steel and tools we are given by
circumstances. Richard Donner and his family were a product of
bad times that made them sick inside. Although that's not their fault
I hate them for it, anyway. You're just plain ol' dead inside and I

don't give a shit about that. Joey, I was minding my own fuckin' business. Getting ready to do whatever with the rest of my life, not at all knowing how much was left and not even caring much about it. My darkness that the story I just told you created left me empty. So, I really have you to thank in a way. You've given me a reason to go on. You've given me a way to lay down my darkness—to fill you with it—that's assuming you have any space left inside you as it's clear to me, now more than ever, that you have your own demons to contend with. I wasn't goin' to do myself nothin'. I was just going to see if fate and nature took me. Then you show up, and now I want to continue on like every other iron fleur-de-lis does in this city."

25

The Tide Turns

It was not much past 6:45am. Maybell had poured her heart out, as well as that whiskey bottle, but it wasn't for Joey's sake, it was for hers.

"Well, the storm is in full swing, now. Sounds like it's blowing away everything not nailed down and tearing up everything else that is. I'm not so sure this house is going to survive, though it has survived all the other storms for the last sixty years or so. I'm going to check the front of the house through the storm door and see if I can tell whatever that was that we heard tear off."

Maybell picked up the bagged Tupperware container, her sister's picture, and then put the gun in her pocket. Grabbing the wet axe from the top of the cage, she looked at the blade as she lifted it, then turned and walked to the hallway. She had to squeeze between the extended ladder from the attic, where she then set the Tupperware and the axe on a stair step.

Joey could see the ladder legs still on the floor and could think of no good reason for her to be packing and storing items like pictures and that book up there. *She must really be impressed with Manson,* he thought. *If I get out of this fucking cage, I'll make her part of a story she won't like as much.* He did admit to himself that she had a gun and an axe, and that would make it a bit more difficult than he wanted.

Joey mumbled from his cage, "So, Mrs. Maybell Johnson, what are you going to do with me?" Maybell stopped moving but let him continue. "Are you going to just leave me in this cage, storm raging outside, see if 'naytcha', as you say, takes me, you and your mutt—keep those hands of yours clean after you dumped all your shit in my head? I mean, did that really do you any good? It's still in you, ya know. It's still all there. You lived it. It will still haunt your thoughts, your dreams, your 'FUTCHA'," he mocked, "You don't really think telling me all that shit gets it outta you, do you? Or maybe you *are* going to kill me. Maybe exact a little revenge on people like me. But you're no different, you're no better. I hear you watching those crime shows. You revel in it. You just never had the courage to play it out. That family, the Donners, they probably never left this city. You were well within your rights to exact your revenge on them. You could have taken those boys out at some point over the years. You could have aimed all that rage outward. Like you did with that old lady, Gadfly. She didn't do shit to you, and you were happy to know she was dead. But you have done nothing but sulk. You're just a nutty ol' bitch now. If you had done your best, you could have taken out that whole fuckin' family. Just set their house on fire or some shit. But, instead, you chose to do nothing."

Maybell had let him say all of that to her back while she was looking at her sister's picture just before putting it in the clear plastic bag. After he had finished, she slowly turned around, tears streaming from her eyes, and rolling in waves down her face when she began to speak.

"No, Mr. Caruso, I couldn't have done all that. It would have darkened me even more. I would have rotted even quicker. You see Joseph, everyone has a chance, several in fact, that come along in their lifetime. Chances at success, chances at love, chances at redemption. What it comes down to is, are you ready and prepared enough to grab hold of one of those chances as they go by. I'm just not like you. Had I done what you suggested, I likely would have rotted in prison or been put to death or, myself, been shot by one of the Donners. No, fate and nature took care of all those things for me. You see, had I exacted any revenge I would have lost my chance at an education. An education that led me to a love most people are never ready for when it shows up. That job at the coffee plant led to me having a chance, a chance I took, to be with Mr. Ronald Johnson. And I certainly wasn't going to empty that darkness into him." Her tears that had dried began to roll again because she mentioned her love.

"Not only that, had I done what you say, then I wouldn't have had a life full of the joy and love that I found with my Ronald. He kept that darkness from even entering my mind. And I wouldn't have had the opportunity to retire in my late thirties. I wouldn't even have had the chance to be with Camille," Cammy clicked up to her and slid her muzzle against Maybell's housecoat in response to her name.

"You see, Mr. Caruso, as angry and nasty as I have been for many years now, it's still about love for me. That, and well, fate and nature work both ways. You're right, that family, the Donners, they went nowhere, and they went nowhere fast. They *did* go on with their lives like nothing had ever happened. And they continued to live in secret lawlessness. Robert Donner got cancer and died two years after the trial. The boys? They took over the shipping business and got popped for tax evasion two years after that. While in the federal pen, one got shanked and died. The other hung himself because he was getting punked every day without any money to protect him. Emily? She was destitute by that point and lost the family home after the business was seized. She used the same gun she killed Sissy with to take her own life on foreclosure day. I went to every funeral held for each one of them. I would just tell Ronald, who was never much of a spiritual man, that I was going to church, and it was true. I did go to church, but not to get the word. I went to get the news; I went to get my closure—though it didn't take. Instead, the revenge fed my darkness. I took pleasure in every one of those funerals.

Maybell paused then sighed, "So, you see, Joe, it comes down to fate and nature taking its course. Most wrongs are righted in the end, though, I don't have much patience. The story I told you was so that I could finally let it go. I never took the chance to confront those boys. The jail likely wouldn't have let me visit them, anyway. If warden had, those little bastards wouldn't have come to the screen just to see my face staring back at them, and they sure wouldn't have listened to anything I had to say."

Maybell looked at her little lamb in the eyes, "Like I said before, you were the representation of that darkness. You were all the Donners wrapped into one package that delivered himself right to my doorstep. You were that chance that comes along occasionally, and I was prepared enough to take that chance. So, I did, and I'm glad that I did. I proved to myself and my sister I am that iron flower, that fleur-de-lis. And I say again, fate and nature will allow one, both, or neither of us to make it through this storm alive. And yes, my hands *will* be clean."

And with that, Maybell turned and went down the hall. Camille dutifully followed her love.

Joey heard Maybell open the front door and then instantly she slammed it shut. The thunderous noise of heavy footfalls and Camille's clicking gallop followed. He kept his eyes trained on the door to the bedroom, fingers pushed through and interlaced tightly around the cage bars, and his face pressed against it so hard it made indentations in his cheeks.

Maybell grabbed the box and axe without breaking her stride and up the ladder she went, cracking one stair with a loud *SNAP* on the way up. A thin metal bar under the stair kept it from breaking totally in half. She quickly caught her balance and up she went— Camille ran up behind her. Joey was more panic stricken than he had ever been. He couldn't conceive of what she was doing nor what it meant for him nor what spooked her at that front door.

His mouth started to part and move closer toward hanging open as Maybell reached down and began to pull the ladder up. Once it was halfway, she was able to stretch out far enough to grab a thin rope that pulled the bottom half of the ladder to a folded position. Once in place, she pulled the rest of the door up. She turned to look down and over to her left so that the two had a direct eyeline to one another. Both had their eyes wide.

Maybell said comedically, "Uh oh."

And that was it, that was the last thing she said as she let squeaky springs and metal brackets do the rest of the talking for her as she let the ceiling door close flush. The string that is used to pull down the attic stairs slowly ascended through the hole it was hung from. Though Joey didn't know it, Maybell took the length of rope and wrapped it around a board that braced the roof then cinched it tight.

"MAYBELL, WHAT THE FUCK IS GOING ON? MAYBELL?" He heard nothing but wind, rain, and the dripping of the water on his head again. But at least now he had choices. None of them, at the moment, seemed like good ones. If he started kicking at the cage, all she had to do was push down the attic door and start shooting. Once he was dead, she could simply chop him up with the axe and dispose of his body piece by piece. He didn't care at all about her sob story. He was convinced now more than ever that she was crazy. She may not be stupid, but he was sure she was totally insane. She may take potshots at him with her pistol just to keep him in the cage and let him dehydrate his way toward death. *That may have been the plan the whole time*, he thought.

Once he fell into her hole, she just used his ears to dump her old worries and irritations into and then would let him die in that cage—at least, that was his belief. But the more he thought about it, none of that made any sense to him. *She could just shoot me and cut me up now.* Unless, in her twisted mind, she believed that her hands really would be clean, and she wouldn't be as bad as him. *That makes the most sense*, he thought. *Yeah, well, I can wait you out, bitch*, he thought further. And just that quick, he wondered still more. *But that doesn't make any sense, either. Why would she just run up the stairs for a storm. It's a storm, sure, but so what? What did she see out there?*

186

Then Joey saw it, too. He saw what Maybell saw. It was seeping through the floorboards.

27

The Tide Rises

It was August 29th, 2005, and although hurricane Katrina had finished much of her wind damage, she was just starting with what she had in store for her finale.

Joseph had no idea when he boarded that plane in Texas that there was a hurricane in the gulf. That's because it wasn't. The hurricane was on the Atlantic side of Florida, and a Texan would have no reason to worry about, nor have much, if any, knowledge of Katrina the week before the storm hit New Orleans head on. The speed bump to the Gulf of Mexico was Florida and they knew about Katrina at that time. Once that bitch had crossed over Florida, all of New Orleans was hopeful she would turn, but it was not to be.

No matter how many times Maybell checked her hurricane updates, almost every four hours for the official ones and intermittently for the regular weather report on the news, in fact, that storm kept coming and refused to go due North until she had set her sights on the Crescent City—so named because of the bowl shape New Orleans is built in. Except for the lip on that bowl of the city that's called the "sliver on the river", not many homes were safe. That "sliver" is where expensive homes sit and many wealthy people reside. The West Bank on the other side of the river got lucky and wasn't flooding. Maybell lived near the Lakefront airport where all the homes in that area would be decimated by mid-day.

All the preparation talk was never about thoughts of self-harm or trying to get to her love, Ronald, in spirit. *If it happens*, she thought, *it happens*. However, she still wanted to be in a place where she controlled her own story all the way to the end. The obit picture and handwritten obituary in the watertight Tupperware were in case she didn't make it out; the baseball card tucked in the paperback was in case she did.

The water was starting to fill up the tray in the bottom of the cage, and his panic turned to desperation. Joey thought he could risk it all and start kicking. He decided he would rather get shot than to die of drowning, and he'd rather die trying than to die a coward.

"MAYBELL, YOU JUS' GONNA LET ME DROWN DOWN HERE?"

She gave no answer and intended to give no quarter.

The wind driven rain and flood waters from a busted levee continued to gurgle up from the floorboards. Joey's time was running shorter, so he made up his mind. He was going to start kicking and if she popped out of the ceiling and started shooting then, so be it, he thought.

Wrapping his fingers tightly on the top of the cage and resting one foot on the bottom, Joey raised his other foot just high enough to kick where the loosened bottom screws were and went to work. He never realized how weak he had gotten until he gave it the first three hard kicks—water sloshing with each strike. His efforts gave him a result of almost nothing. Items on the floor started to float, and the large cinnamon candle fizzled out as a wave lapped over the top.

Joey waited another second, "YOU FUCKING CUNT! YOU'RE REALLY GOING TO DO THIS, NOW AREN'T YOU?" Using his strength to scream up to unsympathetic ears was not wise. He was going to need what little he had in reserve to get out of that cage. Two more kicks resulted in even less than the first three and now the water had started to fill the bottom of the cage to the point where each time he waited, the next kick would have less effect. Water began to topple light furniture; he could hear it all around the house. All the shutter covered windows were holding, and so were the doors, but nothing was keeping the water from seeping into every crack and God-awful crevasse in that house. To add insult to injury, the water from the leak in the roof was still pounding on him. That, and his blood pressure, made his headache return.

Joey lifted himself up to put both feet to work but that was even less effective. He was swinging around like a stunned monkey, and it had nearly no effect at all other than increasing his panic and frustration.

Joey let go of the top of the cage and came down with a splash. Looking at the ceiling, he shouted, "YOU ROTTEN MOTHER FUCKER!"

190

There was no reply at all. It was if he were shouting to a God he didn't believe in but had seen. His god was Maybell Johnson, and she stayed hidden with capricious indifference.

Even with all the storm noise, Maybell could hear Joseph trying to get out of that cage. Though, she could hear her own thoughts, too. She was content with fate and nature taking its course. Sure, she had locked the cage. Leaving it locked even while knowing the storm was coming might have been considered cruel by some, but not Maybell. The cage was locked for her and Camille's safety. The moment he had broken into her house she could have later identified him, and she had no guarantee that he wouldn't come back to kill her to keep that from happening. She was going to turn him in just for that. But once she knew something happened to Gadfly, she decided he would be her vessel to empty her darkness into. If he makes it out, so be it—hands clean. If he survives this flood maybe he decides to give up killing people for a living. *If he dies*, Maybell continued to think, *then it doesn't matter because I already know he's a confessed killer.* Maybell decided at that point it was time to hope for the best and that the rafters would hold so she could make a sandwich.

A third of the cage was now inundated with filthy water. Joey gave the back a few more kicks but all it created were bubbles in the mixture. The wind howled almost as loud as Joey did. All he could hope for now was that he could keep his nose above the water and that the house was high enough above sea level that he could survive there until someone found him and that was as unlikely as one could imagine. The number of houses were vast and if this one was flooding so were hundreds, even thousands more.

That's when his life began to flash before his eyes. If he would have seen those images while completely safe and free from harm or threat of death, they would have mattered none to him. But knowing one is likely going to die has a way of chemically changing lack of care and concerns for our lifetime actions into deeply felt regrets, sadness, darkness.

None of what he saw, felt, nor experienced in that split-second View-Master moment would have been considered by anyone as positive. The only positive he had done in his life was negligible and even that was only when he was a child. Regardless, he saw none of that. Instead, all of *his* darkness was there.

The few relationships that no one would ever call romantic were there. The violence that enveloped all those plastic and self-centered connections to others he had encountered appeared as if in a fever dream. The daughter he only saw but twice and never talked about, popped in his head and sat with a frown. A vision of his mother's body after she overdosed in the bathroom was next. She was the only person who took up for him no matter his wrongdoing and never questioned his intentions. In that microsecond he realized that her actions partially made him the way he was—a narcissist. The beatings he endured at the hands of his alcoholic father, Joey felt every one of those again, several dozens of them, in fact. The schoolyard bullying, kids making fun of him and his ragged clothes, those feelings came flooding in.

The vision of the day his father was in handcuffs in the back of a squad car, it was there. The feelings he had of abandonment when he was twelve returned and felt just as bad as it did when he was hit in the head by "Bertha". Maybell was there and her face looked the way it did when she scared him the most. She had an axe in her hand and casting her chilling eyes into his. It was her signature Kubrickian stare.

Everyone he ever tortured and killed for money, or for any other reason, they were all there, too, and they all shared that same Maybell expression.

The choices he didn't take to make a positive change in his life; each one was laid out before him in rapid succession. The choices he did make that were for his benefit and his benefit alone were spread out like playing cards, including the jokers, too, as the water rose.

Joey got on his knees, though it was not in prayer for forgiveness. Instead, it was an attempt to keep his nose above the water as it neared the top of the cage. Within those several minutes, the water had gotten high enough that now he needed to keep his nostrils outside of the cage wire to survive a few more minutes. His breathing was cut off every time a wave pushed in from nowhere.

The cage began to slide, and it gave Joey the most hope he had since the putrid liquid began to seep in. He was disoriented, though, after his end-of-life scare and had no idea of which way was up. If he could have, Joey would have clapped with joy as if he had seen a great movie with a fantastic ending. But the cage was not moving in any direction, nor in any way, that would help him. It was sliding closer to the back of the house and into deeper water. The cage was sliding because the cinderblock stilts that kept the house and him at the peak of where he needed to be to keep breathing were no longer of any value. The house was being pushed off and to the right side. The blocks that once held up the rear were giving way. The wind driven water surge had taken its toll on the house that had survived all other storms. The Widow Johnson's home was going down by the transom and was already half full of water.

Maybell never got to that sandwich. She was holding on to the rafters as the house began to shift. She had never wanted to live so badly in the last fifteen years as she did in this moment. Her life flashed before her eyes as it did Joey's. Though she would never come to know it from his point of view, her life images were much different than his.

She heard Jamielynn and Momma singing happy birthday when she had turned six. She saw her momma laughing at her while she took the faux dinner order. Her sister's flour covered face flashed before her, smiling, as she burned her first cake. The smell of it was there, too, and it was heavenly.

Maybell, although hanging on to a sinking house, was beaming as she saw another cake, the one from the picture, the one at her wedding. Then she saw moving images of her and Ronald dancing as family and friends clapped and cheered. She saw both of his promotion ceremonies and the celebrations that followed. She saw the first day that she met Camille in her front yard. The few but cherished friends she had since childhood were shown in several tender emotional moments. There were scenes of their birthday parties, graduations, christenings, and baptisms of the children of her and Ronald's family and friends.

Maybell saw, in an instant, every embrace her and Ronald ever shared. She saw him lean down from somewhere above her and kiss her on the forehead. He said her favorite words, "That's my little Mrs. May." It was like hearing the best symphony ever written, every note perfection. Maybell was sobbing uncontrollably,

194

but not in sadness. She felt like she had won a billion-dollar lottery and everyone she had ever lost was whole again.

Then she heard Ronald say, *You can't kill bad grass, girl, you're going to live so much longer. You ain't bent them corners, did ya?* Maybell appeared to be like a person struggling with bipolar disorder and in the middle of a mixed episode as her tears turned into laughter.

Her vision of Ronald laughed too and spoke one final time as his image faded, saying, *I love you, Mrs. May. I always have and I will for an eternity.*

Her Jamielynn appeared and said, *You're an Iron fleur-de-lis and you will survive like all the rest of them iron flowers do.* And with that, her end-of-life visions concluded just as quickly as they had begun.

She grabbed the shaking Camille and re-clung to that rafter brace even though it felt as if it would give way at any moment. And although to the rest of New Orleans—the rest that stayed that August 28 and 29th of 2005—it was a noisy hell, everything went completely quiet and still for Maybell. It was in that instant that she knew her darkness was gone. She realized she saw none of it during her absolute love story of a vision.

In a snap back to reality for both the reformed anti-heroine and the criminal, they both felt the house as it slid far back enough where the blocks toppled over like a few dominos in a line. And with that final act of "naytcha'", as Maybell would say, things in that little part of the world were set right. Maybell's darkness was now cast out for good, the one that had been within her and the one now below her.

Joseph Lee Caruso's cage came down slowly, slid toward the vanity that had already turned and blocked the back exit he had once visualized as his path to freedom, and laid to rest on the bottom of Mr. and Mrs. Johnson's bedroom floor—the cage he had built with the tools and supplies given to him by others.

Maybell had escaped her cage with the key Joseph had unwittingly given to her. Joey wasn't a lamb; he was a wolf. More than that, he was a mirror. And when Maybell looked into that mirror, it frightened her to see how dark she had become.

When people die, they take the memory of those they have with them. It makes those lost to tragedy die a little more each time those that loved them pass on, too. It's even more of a tragedy if they take their own life due to the sorrow of the loss of that loved one. Everyone has moments when only they and the person with them were part of that conversation—that laugh, that consolation, that tender shared moment. It's gone when they are, because no one else was around to see it. If we are alive, then so is a little piece of the ones we cared about. That's what gave Maybell the will to be that Iron Iris, to continue, to live on and thrive and keep the memory of those she had lost vivid; to fulfill who she was to Ronald, his Little Mrs. May.

28

The Rise Of The Reformed Anti-Heroine

It was as hot as Maybell could ever remember feeling since her "flashes" during menopause. It was the next morning, and the rain had subsided. Maybell sat in her crooked shambles of a house, perched high above her marital bed and a dead cold-blooded killer in a cage below. Maybell took a Coke and the gallon jug of water from the icy bath in the cooler. After dipping a towel in the ice water, Maybell mopped every part of her body that didn't have clothes on it. Then, with the second dip, she wet her clothes down as well. Camille simply drank from the ice water in the cooler. The house was tilted to the point that the bowl would be too shallow on the edge and rendered it useless, anyway. Maybell shrugged and let Camille go at it.

It was time to get out of the sweltering attic. The storm was hours gone and the flood waters settled to their highest peak. However, she decided she would eat a PB&J before picking up that well sharpened axe that was never intended for Joey. She smiled to herself as she got to that sandwich, after all.

"Camille, I sho' am gonna miss that fucka'," she said as she gave her companion a pat on the head. "Naaaa, not really. I'd miss Gadfly first," she chuckled as she pulled out two slices of bread from the half-eaten loaf and made that PB&J, one she shared with Cammy. She started to hear the helicopters overhead that were dropping sandbags to block the flow of water pouring through the gaping hole of a nearby levee.

That was her cue.

Maybell retrieved the axe that had slid all the way to the other side of the attic during all the hell and high water. She picked the spot that was weakened by the continuous water that had been pouring in and leaking on the Joey's head. With a few good swings, daylight emerged. She made short work of it, and it was at just the right height for her to come out of if she added more elevation by using the cooler as a step. She would then, of course, reach back in and pluck Cammy out.

After about ten minutes of chopping, she was able to make a hole big enough to pull herself through. Maybell used the axe to cut a length of rope and tied it to the handle of the water jug. She flung the rope on the outside of the hole. Then she took what was left of the thin cord and tied it around herself with the container holding her chance at a new life tucked in her waistband. Camille watched as Maybell slid over the ice chest, pull two sodas out, and put them in her pockets. After closing the lid, standing on top, and with a short hop, she pulled herself up and out. Then she pulled the rope she had tossed outside and pulled the water jug up. Cammy whined and hopped up and down on her front paws showing fear that her love would leave her there.

Maybell's face appeared in the hole, "Aww, now girl you know betta' than that. Momma ain't gone leave you nowhere. Now com'on heya," she said as she put both hands though the hole. With one hop, Camille made it to Maybell's hands. She was able to catch Cammy midair under her full-grown puppy's front shoulders and latched her thumbs underneath, pulling her through the hole and sat her on the rooftop.

They both stopped to catch their breath. Another 'copter was overhead, so Maybell shielded her eyes with one hand and waved with the other that had a white towel in it then instantly she collapsed. The adrenalin dump, heat exposure, and loss of electrolytes had wiped out Maybell. Her heart didn't have all of what it needed to pump correctly. Camille barked and whined and walked around Maybell's head in a semi-circle. Cammy continued to pace, bark, whine, and lick her momma's face.

"Girl, what's wrong wit' 'chu?" Maybell asked as she came back to life. After realizing that she was laid flat, Maybell asked aloud, "Lawd, what's wrong with me? How long was I out, baby?" Maybell picked up the jug of water and drank as much as she could before coughing and sputtering. The idea of jumping into that filthy water below crossed Maybell's mind as she looked around to see if she could see anyone coming to rescue her—could be hours, days, or after death she thought. While scanning the waterline, the widow was fairly sure she saw a body floating about a hundred and fifty yards out. She abandoned the idea of jumping into the water below to keep cool. Then she thought she was crazy for even considering it because Cammy would have had none of that, anyway, and she would never leave her love on that roof. An hour later, one boat from the Cajun Navy, as they would become known the world over after the storm, showed up.

"Boy this ol' lady and her dog sure is glad y'all came from out yonder. My my, it looks like da' lawd done answered my prayers. And jus' in time, too," Maybell crowed.

"Yes ma'am! You lucky to be alive. Yes indeed! Come over to this side where the roof is closer to the water by the back. We gon' pick you and your pooch up from there."

"Yes sir, you got that right. Come on here, girl, let's go get ourselves rescued!"

The small aluminum boat and an even smaller horsepower motor that carried two men ferried to the back side of the house. They would never know how close they were to the murderer of Mrs. Dorthy Gadfly.

Maybell made her way to the back of the house and Cammy clicked along with her. Her tail wagged like she was about to get ice cream from Maybell's spoon, as she had so many times over the years. After settling into the boat, they gave Maybell a life jacket.

"I'm Donald and this here is my brother Larry. What's your name, Ms…"

"Ms. Townson. Ms. Jamielynn Townson."

"Pleasure to meet you, Ms. Townson. Okay, hold on, it'll be a long ride. And if I tell you not to look, shut your eyes. I don't want you to see nothin' that you can't unsee, if you know what I mean."

"Oh, I promise you, Donald…may I call you Donald?"

"Absolutely, ma'am!"

"Donald, I've seen enough to last a lifetime. I ain't need see no more."

Larry spoke up, "I know dat's right."

The four started out toward the lowering sun and left a mystery or two behind.

Epilogue

One More Dig After Darkness

Somewhere, but not just anywhere in America, there was a television on and tuned to CNN. It was a television in Chicago, Illinois. And on that television was yet another news story regarding the fifth anniversary of Katrina. It was a story of all the lives lost, some of the people who still morn those losses, and a few mysteries that the storm waters would never give up.

One, in particular, being a cold case involving a man's body found locked in a cage in a flooded house. A cage in a house that was destroyed by Katrina's flood waters from a broken levee. The house, the FBI Special Agent from the New Orleans field office who was being interviewed noted, was owned by a Mr. Ronald and Mrs. Maybell Johnson. Mr. Johnson had died several years before the storm hit, and Mrs. Johnson's body had never been recovered.

The reporter went on to ask, "Special Agent Williams, what makes this cold case so intriguing? We have heard many horror stories bout bodies being found, and some that were never found, correct?"

"Yes, ma'am, that is absolutely correct. However, there are two things that make this an interesting case. The first being that the man in the cage was on the FBI's radar as a hired gun. We found he did a few stints in jail for petty theft, domestic violence, a gun charge in his mid-twenties and so on. That was known before I joined the bureau. He actually had his wallet and ID still in his back pocket when his body was found a week after the floodwaters were pumped out of New Orleans. Through DNA we positively identified him. Then we were able to run an exhaustive search of internet traffic the last few weeks leading up to the storm and found he had agreed to complete a hit on Mrs. Johnson's, neighbor. To say his past was checkered would be an understatement. I'm not allowed to get into any active criminal investigations, but it appears he…" Agent Williams looked directly into the TV screen and accentuated her next word, "…MAY have been in New Orleans for nefarious reasons."

"The second interesting fact that continues to intrigue us at the bureau is that this picture," Williams held up the photograph of Maybell in her all-red blazer and perfect makeup. The camera slowly zoomed in on her face with her knowing grin in all its eight-by-ten glory as Special Agent Williams continued, "and its accompanying obituary of Maybell Johnson, one that mind you, was not written by the Times Picayune, showed up two weeks later in their offices. Full disclosure, I interviewed Ms. Johnson when I was New Orleans officer during the Dorthy Gadfly investigation that, as some of your viewers may remember, was stymied by Katrina and is yet to be closed. The two, as I mentioned earlier—Gadfly and Johnson—were next door neighbors."

"Special Agent Williams, let me make sure I understand. The obituary of the woman who owned the house that the man in the cage was found in shows up two weeks after the storm?"

"Correct."

"And you noted at the top of the interview that she was a widow, correct?

"Correct."

"I was reading about this case, and she had no children and no family to speak of, correct?"

"That is also correct."

"Special Agent Williams, who would have been the one to send in the picture and the obituary and, more importantly, where is Maybell Johnson?"

Williams thought to herself, *The fuck if I know but I can't wait to be the one to catch her ass.*

"Let me answer the last question first: We don't know where Mrs. Johnson is and all attempts to locate her have been, up to this point, exhausted," Williams trailed off in her thought process again for a microsecond as she visualized the garbage can that, had she been quicker in thought and less surprised in emotion, she would have just pulled the gray bag liner and looked. Airtime being expensive and viewership fickle, caused the reporter to quickly ask, "Do you have any idea who sent in the obituary of a woman who has never been found, dead nor alive?"

The fit woman watching the story, while laying on her bed in yoga pants and a white button-down blouse with an elderly

204

overweight dog at her side, giggled as she watched her old nemesis have to stoop to the public's help to find her with five years already gone.

"Well, that is the most interesting and even comical part of this case, if there is one."

"And what possibly could that be, Special Agent Williams?"

"The postmark was from Texas."

"Oh, why is that significant?"

Williams looked into the camera again and said flatly, "The return address was that of Joseph Lee Caruso, the man in the cage."

www.ingramcontent.com/pod-product-compliance
Lightning Source LLC
Chambersburg PA
CBHW011508170626
46812CB00009B/3019